AF581142

It was a *body*.

A woman. Lying there frozen in place, the angle of her limbs so awkward she had to be dead.

Horror flooded Sky's system. Then the man moved, lunging toward her. She bolted, panic driving her toward the trees. Only one thought filled her mind: *Get away.* She could hear him coming after her.

She stumbled and nearly went down but caught herself on a tree. Behind her, the man grunted. She dared a glance back to see the flat blade of the shovel swinging toward her head. She managed to dodge it seconds before the shovel hit the tree with a reverberating clang.

Adrenaline drove her forward despite the terror raking her inside. Suddenly, Sky slammed into a climber before she could grind to a halt. A pair of arms wrapped around her and Sky looked up at her unsuspecting rescuer. Relief crashed through her harder than spring runoff over Yosemite Falls.

Kellie VanHorn is an award-winning author of inspirational romance and romantic suspense. She has college degrees in biology and nautical archaeology, but her sense of adventure is most satisfied by a great story. When not writing, Kellie can be found homeschooling her four children, camping, baking and gardening. She lives with her family in western Michigan.

Books by Kellie VanHorn

Love Inspired Suspense

Fatal Flashback
Buried Evidence
Hunted in the Wilderness
Dangerous Desert Abduction
Treacherous Escape
Wyoming Ranch Sabotage

Park Ranger Agents

Ambushed in Yosemite

Visit the Author Profile page at LoveInspired.com.

AMBUSHED IN YOSEMITE

KELLIE VANHORN

If you purchased this book without a cover you should be aware that this book is stolen property. It was reported as "unsold and destroyed" to the publisher, and neither the author nor the publisher has received any payment for this "stripped book."

Recycling programs for this product may not exist in your area.

ISBN-13: 978-1-335-91906-9

Ambushed in Yosemite

Copyright © 2026 by Kellie VanHorn

All rights reserved. No part of this book may be used or reproduced in any manner whatsoever without written permission.

Without limiting the exclusive rights of any author, contributor or the publisher of this publication, any unauthorized use of this publication to train generative artificial intelligence (AI) technologies is expressly prohibited. Harlequin also exercises their rights under Article 4(3) of the Digital Single Market Directive 2019/790 and expressly reserves this publication from the text and data mining exception.

This is a work of fiction. Names, characters, places and incidents are either the product of the author's imagination or are used fictitiously. Any resemblance to actual persons, living or dead, businesses, companies, events or locales is entirely coincidental.

For questions and comments about the quality of this book, please contact us at CustomerService@Harlequin.com.

® is a trademark of Harlequin Enterprises ULC.

Love Inspired
22 Adelaide St. West, 41st Floor
Toronto, Ontario M5H 4E3, Canada
www.LoveInspired.com

HarperCollins Publishers
Macken House, 39/40 Mayor Street Upper,
Dublin 1, D01 C9W8, Ireland
www.HarperCollins.com

Printed in Lithuania

1 2 3 4 5 6 7 8 9 10 LIT 28 27 26 25

I will lift up mine eyes unto the hills, from whence cometh my help. My help cometh from the Lord, which made heaven and earth.

—*Psalm* 121:1–2

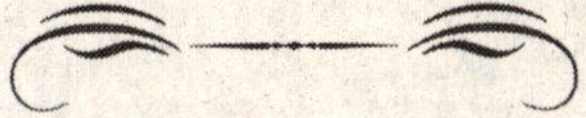

For Lee and Marsha

With heartfelt gratitude to
Kerry Johnson, Ali Herring, Katie Gowrie
and the amazing Love Inspired team at Harlequin.

ONE

A chilly, late-May breeze whisked stray leaves across the road and kicked up mini dust devils as Skylar Jansen jogged past the Yosemite Valley Nature Center. She brushed loose strands of red hair out of her eyes and glanced at her watch. Six fifteen a.m. Plenty of time to check the trail again and take a quick shower before she needed to report to work.

Ahead, ambitious hikers moved like tiny ants up the cliff face along Vernal Falls, working their way up to the cables on the summit of Half Dome before any of the area's notorious afternoon thunderstorms might catch them off guard. Maybe eventually she'd summon the courage to try the ascent herself. There were plenty of ways to get hurt—or vanish—in this park, as she knew from personal experience.

But none of that mattered because of the awe-inspiring views. This was why she'd upended her life and left her high-paying, high-stress career in New York City for a low-paying job as a seasonal interpretive ranger with the National Park Service—to get in touch with nature again by talking about it with visitors as an educator. Well, that was *one* of the reasons she'd left New York. Being dumped by her long-time boyfriend might've had something to do with it, too.

She veered off the road a short distance past the nature

center, taking a trail that ran deeper into one of the Valley's many granite climbing areas. She'd love to get out here with climbing gear one day. After years of indoor gyms, the idea of tackling a real rock face sounded both exhilarating and terrifying at the same time. Birds twittered to each other in the tree branches high above, and the breeze carried a fresh, earthy scent she'd missed during her years in New York City.

Sky slowed her pace, scanning the trees ahead for the path she wanted, then ducked around the decaying wood post marking the entrance. Her pulse kicked up a notch, the same way it did every time she set foot on this trail, even though she'd already walked it a dozen times since her arrival. Her father had vanished out here eighteen years ago, and despite all the search teams and anonymous tips and reward offers, no trace of him had been found.

Please, Lord, let today be different...

She eyed the ground as she went, keeping her pace slow so she wouldn't miss anything. Of course, it was a fool's errand. Why should she find something now, after all this time? But hope fluttered in her chest anyway, mixed with the ever-present fear that she actually *would* find some clue they'd missed.

Then she'd have to confront her father's death as fact rather than theory.

The wind rustled the leaves around her, sending a chill across her arms. It had taken her a few weeks in Yosemite before she'd mustered up the courage to walk this path, the last place witnesses had seen him. He'd worked as a law enforcement ranger here for years, and even after he'd lost his left leg below the knee in an accident, he'd never let a prosthesis slow him down. He'd loved climbing and had taken every opportunity to tackle a few pitches after his shift ended. Until one day, when he didn't come home.

A granite face rose up in front of her, part of the Glacier Point apron. Nobody was out here yet, but by midmorning there would probably be a dozen amateur climbers trying these easier routes. Working their way up to attempting El Capitan.

Had her father stopped here to climb? Or had he pressed farther into the Illilouette Gorge? Search teams had combed the area for weeks after his disappearance, but they'd never found so much as a boot print. When a witness came forward saying they'd spotted him getting into a car with an unidentified woman, too many people had accepted the easy answer. But not Sky. She knew her dad. He'd loved the Lord and her mom and their family, and he never would've left them. No matter what the media believed. She checked her watch. Thirty minutes before she had to turn back. That left enough time to try one of the many side trails she hadn't walked yet.

She had to pick her way more carefully back here, farther off the beaten paths of the front country walked by four million visitors a year. The only feet treading these trails belonged to climbers and the odd park employee looking to escape the crowds, leaving the route harder to make out. Branches stretched spindly fingers toward her, scratching exposed skin on her legs. Maybe running shorts hadn't been the best call this morning.

Water from the nearby river gurgled in the distance, and the shadows deepened as she passed deeper into the woods. She paused, glancing behind her to make sure she could still see the trail. That would be a great way to start her summer out here as a new ranger—getting lost and forcing Yosemite Search and Rescue to waste valuable resources looking for her. When she faced forward again, goose bumps popped on her arms. Was that a shadow moving between the trees?

Sky froze, then forced in a breath and kept going. It was probably just an animal out hunting for breakfast. Her chest tightened far too easily these days, thanks to the burnout and adrenal fatigue brought on by her advertising career in New York. But she was going to retrain herself to enjoy life again. Like taking deep breaths of this beautiful, fresh mountain air and placing one foot in front of another despite the rigid tension in her shoulders.

Sunlight glinted off the water between the trees to her left as she entered a small clearing. California poppies danced red and black among the grasses. She'd taken two steps out into the sun when she paused, lifting a hand to shield her eyes in the bright morning light and stifling a gasp.

Someone was there, hard to see in black clothing beneath the shadow of the trees, a few paces to the left of the path and maybe twenty feet away from her. He was standing still, almost like he hoped she wouldn't notice him. A greeting rose to her lips before she realized he held a shovel. *What?* Was he out collecting soil samples or something? He wasn't dressed in any uniform she recognized, and a ball cap was pulled so low over his face she couldn't make out his features.

"Excuse me." Sky waved her other hand, pasting a smile on her face. She preferred to appear friendly when confronting unruly visitors. "Good morning. You know you're not supposed to be digging in a national park, right?"

The man lifted the shovel, clutching the metal handle against his chest, and took a step sideways. What was that on the ground behind him? "I'm on staff here. Doing trail maintenance." His voice sounded strained, like maybe he wasn't using his natural tone. And the way the words came out carefully measured made uneasiness buzz through her system like a wasp looking for someone to sting. "My name's Jeremy. Who are you?"

What trail was he working on, ten feet off a path? She strained to see past him, to see what he'd been doing. A mound of dirt lay piled to one side of him, as if he were digging a hole. Or filling one. Either way, something felt very off. And what was that red object on the ground? A jacket he'd cast aside?

"I'm a ranger." She backed up a step. Maybe he'd think she was in law enforcement and carried a gun. She'd heard stories about some of the seasonal workers that came through here. They weren't *all* college students or thirty-somethings escaping high-stress careers. If she turned and ran, would he be fast enough to catch her? Or was she completely blowing things out of proportion? She pulled out her cell phone to make a show of checking the time. "I need to get back to my shift now. Nice to meet you."

She waved, then backed up another step, preparing to pivot and bolt down the path as soon as she left the clearing.

"Wait." The word came out harsh, edged with an undertone of command that made her flinch. The man still clutched that shovel to his chest as he stepped out of the shadows. The morning sun streaking over the mountains kept his face hidden. "You didn't tell me *your* name."

His tone sent a chill raking down her arms. They both stood frozen for a moment, as if balanced on a teeter-totter that might drop in either direction with the slightest motion. Then her gaze landed on the red jacket behind him, and her lungs filled with concrete. That wasn't just a jacket—

It was a *body*.

A woman, from the long dark hair draped across the

ground. Lying there frozen in place, the angle of her limbs so awkward she had to be dead.

Horror flooded Sky's system, lodging her feet to the ground like they were rooted in place. Then the man moved, sprinting toward her. She bolted, panic driving her across the clearing and into the trees so blindly she didn't know if she'd found the right path or not. Only one thought filled her mind: *Get away.*

Her feet pounded the packed ground as she scanned ahead, dodging exposed tree roots and ducking around low-hanging limbs. Above the thrum of her heart in her ears and the gasping whooshes of her breath, she could hear him coming after her with a rustle of fabric and thudding footsteps.

She stumbled and nearly went down but caught herself against a nearby trunk, rough bark biting into her palms. Behind her, the man grunted. She dared a glance back to see the flat blade of the shovel swinging toward her head. Her heart barreled into her throat, threatening to choke her, but she managed to push away from the tree seconds before the shovel hit the trunk with a reverberating clang.

She had no idea where the path had gone or where she was heading. And was the man still chasing her? A granite slab loomed above the trees up ahead, and she angled toward it. One of the climbing pitches, closer to the main road. Adrenaline drove her forward, despite the burning in her lungs and terror raking her insides. Then the trees spit her out into a clearing in front of the granite pitch, and she slammed into a climber before she could grind to a halt. A pair of warm, solid arms wrapped around her, keeping her from losing her balance.

Sky looked up at her unsuspecting rescuer, and relief crashed through her harder than spring runoff over Yosemite Falls. She'd never met him in person, but she'd seen his face nearly every day as she passed the wall of full-time staff pictures on her way into the Visitor Center: Bode Tucker, Investigative Services Branch, or ISB for short. One of the four NPS Special Agents who worked on a special crimes task force out of Yosemite.

His lips twisted into a smile like he was about to make a joke until his blue eyes latched on to her face. The fear siphoning out of her system made her whole body tremble, and as a sob worked its way up into her throat, she pressed her forehead against his chest and let the tears streak down her cheeks.

Bode Tucker awkwardly patted the back of the crying woman in his arms, letting the climbing harness he'd been about to put on fall to the ground. The top of her head barely reached his collarbone. He glanced around the trail, his gaze settling on the trees in the direction she'd come from. Maybe she was a visitor who'd gotten lost and just found her way out? She was dressed in running clothes, and her red hair was neatly tucked back in a ponytail with no sign of twigs or debris, nothing to suggest she'd been out overnight.

"Hey, are you okay?"

She pulled away from him, swiping her hands over her cheeks. When she turned soft gray-green eyes up at him, an unwelcome flicker of awareness darted through his insides. She looked close to his own age, maybe late twenties or early thirties. Freckles danced across her nose and cheeks, and her lips were pink and full—but natural, not coated in makeup.

"I'm sorry." She glanced behind her, then around the clearing. Her movements were jerky, her shoulders rigid.

Whatever had happened, she'd been terrified. When she kept talking, her words came tumbling out. "I didn't mean to crash into you, but there was a man who claimed he was doing trail maintenance, only he wasn't. He was burying a body, and he came after me—" A sob hiccupped from her chest.

"Whoa." Bode ducked his head to try to catch her eye. "Say that again. What happened? Did you say there was a body?"

Her gaze locked with his, and as he took a deep breath, she mirrored his movement. Good. If she calmed down, maybe he could figure out what had happened.

"We need to call in a report," she said between gasps. "I ran into a man back there, digging near the river. There was a woman—" She broke off, checking over her shoulder again. Her voice dropped to a whisper. "Did you hear that?"

Bode stared past her to the woods she'd just left. Wind rustled through the treetops, and a stick cracked somewhere close by. Could be an animal. Or it could be her assailant... He frowned. "Let's head back to the trail."

He gestured toward the path he'd taken from the front country trail, then dug his phone out of his pocket as he followed a pace behind her. Just as he paused to tap past his lock screen, a loud pop sounded from the forest to his right. At almost the same moment, a high-pitched whine zipped past his face, exactly where his head would've been if he hadn't stopped.

The woman—he still didn't know her name—screamed, and he dived forward, tackling her to the ground, as more pops sounded.

"Go! Go!" He positioned himself between her and the shooter as they got up on hands and knees and scrambled toward the cover of the trees. The cool shadows of the woods enveloped them, and Bode jumped to his feet, tugging her up with him. He pointed at the narrow path ahead. “That way.”

She nodded, eyes wide, then burst into a run. He followed hard on her heels, listening for the sound of more gunfire or the thump of footsteps behind them, but their assailant seemed to have vanished back into the forest. A few minutes later, they burst out onto the wide, pine-straw covered trail that led back to the nature center. The woman clutched her side, breathing hard, but jogged alongside him as he angled toward the road.

Only once they were safely out of the trees did he stop to catch his breath.

“Are you hurt?” He scanned her from head to toe but didn’t see any obvious signs of injury, just some smudges of dirt and scratches on her legs and arms.

She shook her head. “I’m okay. Just shaken up. You?”

“I’m fine.” That first bullet had barely missed him. *Thank You, God.* Harper, his three-year-old daughter, didn’t need to lose her only remaining parent. “I’m Special Agent Bode Tucker, part of the Investigative Services Branch of the National Park Service.” He gestured down at his blue T-shirt and gray athletic pants. “I’m afraid you’ll have to take my word for it, since I’m out of uniform.”

An early morning climb was a rare pleasure, between solo-parenting Harper ever since his wife’s passing and juggling his caseload. The Yosemite Valley childcare center that cared for his daughter during the day opened early a couple of days a week, so he took advantage when he could. Thankfully, Harper loved her teachers, a fact that lessened some of his dad-guilt.

“I know who you are.” The woman offered him a shaky smile. “I’m a new interpretive ranger. Seasonal. My name’s

Skylar Jansen, but you can call me Sky. I've seen your picture in the Visitor Center." Her cheeks colored prettily. "Thanks for your help back there."

Jansen. Same name as one of their longest-standing cold cases—a ranger who'd vanished several years ago. A light bulb clicked on in his mind. "You're Andy Jansen's daughter, aren't you? I heard you were hired this season." He didn't usually give much credit to gossip, but in his line of work, it paid to listen. And when a missing ranger's daughter was hired at the same park, everyone was bound to know before long.

She nodded, a shadow crossing her face. That was something they had in common. Like him, she too knew loss. He offered his hand. "Nice to meet you, Sky." He held up the phone he'd managed to keep fisted during their impromptu run. "I'll call this in and get us a ride."

Fifteen minutes later, Bode led the way into park headquarters to the small office space shared by the ISB agents. After flipping on the lights, he showed Sky to a seat, then called Chief Ranger Roger Kleinman to give him a brief overview of what had happened.

"He wants us to meet him at his office in fifteen minutes," he told her after he hung up. "Law enforcement rangers are on the way to the scene. Can I get you a drink? Coffee? Water?"

"Just water. My nerves don't need coffee yet." She ran her fingers along her forehead, brushing loose strands of ginger hair out of her face. "I should notify my supervisor I'll be late." But after reaching into one of her pockets, she froze. "My phone's gone. I must've dropped it."

"We'll find it," he reassured her, more to keep her calm than because finding a lost cell phone in the wilderness would be easy. He'd need to go back and collect his climbing gear, too.

He grabbed her a drink and was just about to call his own supervisor when she walked in. Special-Agent-in-Charge Reese Henlow had been the one who recruited him into the ISB after working with him on several search-and-rescue operations. The petite, blond-haired woman in her mid-thirties didn't look particularly ferocious, but she was a force to be reckoned with. And in all honesty, she'd probably saved his life. After his wife, Isla, had died of cancer when Harper was only six months old, Bode had nearly drowned in the flood of his grief. If Reese and the rest of the team hadn't been there, supporting him and keeping him involved with new cases, he might not have pulled through the way he had.

"Bode, you're here early." Reese waved as she set her bag down next to her desk. Then her gaze flitted to Sky, and one side of her mouth lifted in a half smirk as she glanced back at him. "And who did you bring with you?"

Warmth surged up the back of his neck. Sometime in the last six months, after the two-year anniversary of Isla's passing, Reese had decided it was time for Bode to move forward—regardless of what *he* thought about the matter.

He stuffed his hands in his pockets and kept his face neutral. "This is Sky. She's a seasonal interp who unfortunately ran into some trouble this morning." *And I don't mean me.*

Reese's expression immediately shifted into a look of sympathy that reflected her heart for supporting victims of crime. "What happened?" She glanced between the two of them.

Sky let out a slow breath, but Bode couldn't help noticing the way her leg bounced. Or how she played with the bottom hem of her shirt. Was it nerves? The aftereffects of adrenaline? "I went out for an early morning jog near the nature center and veered off onto a backcountry trail along the Illilouette. A man was out there digging where he wasn't supposed to be. It took me a minute to see, but he was—" she grimaced "—burying someone."

Reese shot Bode a sharp glance, and he nodded. Homicide in the national park. Yeah, this case was going to be a big deal.

"I ran for it. The man chased me until I happened upon Agent Tucker." Her face softened as she looked at him, and warmth flared in his chest. *This* was why he did this job—to help people like Sky.

He turned his attention back to Reese just in time to catch the look on her face as she glanced between them. *Great.* Who knew what ideas she was entertaining? He cleared his throat. "The perp opened fire on us. He must've had a suppressor on that gun, because it wasn't very loud."

"Sounds like this might end up being our case." Reese shifted some files on her desk. "Which means *your* case, Bode, because Jace and Graham are tied up, and I'm leaving for Canyonlands in a few days."

With fewer than three dozen ISB agents covering the entire National Park Service, their small task force always had something demanding their attention. Even if Bode didn't have an active case going, the western parks like Yosemite had more than their share of cold cases. As Reese spoke, Sky glanced his way with her brows just slightly raised, an expression of hopefulness that tugged at him. Maybe because he was the one who'd first helped her, she seemed grateful to have his presence a little longer.

"You got it, boss." He gave Reese a mock salute. "I'll discuss it with Kleinman. We have a meeting now." He turned to Sky. "Ready?" When she nodded, he led the way to the door.

"Sure." Reese waved them out, and a few minutes later, they arrived at the chief ranger's office.

Roger Kleinman, an older man nearing the end of his tenure with the NPS, propped his elbows on the desk and tented his fingers as Sky explained what had happened. "Did you get a look at the assailant? Any kind of description you can give us will help."

She scrubbed her hands over her face. "He was male, average height. Maybe five foot nine or ten? Slim, wiry build. I never saw his face. He told me he worked for trail maintenance, but he might've been lying. Said his name was… Jared? No… Jeremy. That was it. I didn't notice the—" her throat bobbed "—body until after I'd already talked to him."

The chief ranger scribbled notes as she spoke, then reached for his phone when she was done. "Thank you, Ranger Jansen. I'll get in touch with the sheriff's office and the FBI satellite office. Agent Tucker, are you taking lead for the ISB?"

"Yes, sir. I'll head over to the scene as soon as I escort Ranger Jansen back to her home. Did the rangers find the victim?"

Kleinman nodded. "But I can fill you in on the details later." When his gaze flicked to Sky, she shook her head.

"Please, sir, I want to know. Was she dead?"

He watched her for a moment, perhaps debating how much to say. "Yes. From initial observations, the victim was female, early twenties. Cause of death appears to be strangulation. The body was still in rigor mortis."

"So, time of death less than twenty-four hours," Bode supplied. His brain began collating a list of all the things he'd need to do: contact the FBI and sheriff's office, gather evidence, check the missing persons database…

Sky's forehead crinkled as she listened. "Was she taken from the park?"

"We don't know yet," Kleinman said. "No missing persons have been reported matching the physical description, but we need to cross-check with other agencies."

Bode turned to Sky. "Let's get you home. You can take a few days off, if you need them. I'll clear it with your supervisor." He didn't know where she was from, but doubtless a little time away would help after what she'd gone through.

"Absolutely," the chief ranger added. "That won't be a problem at all."

Sky drew in a ragged breath as she stood. "No, I'd like to get to work. The routine will be helpful." She headed for the door, and Bode followed but stopped when Kleinman gestured him back.

The chief ranger pressed his fingers to his temple, then spoke softly as if he didn't want her to hear from out in the hall. "Tucker, the victim was missing an earring. In its place was a carabiner."

What? "A carabiner? Like for climbing?"

"Yeah. Clipped through the earlobe."

Something twisted in his gut. No woman clipped a carabiner to her own ear. And if her attacker had done it… That was classic serial killer behavior.

He chewed silently on the information as he walked Sky the short distance back to her seasonal housing in the Valley. The man had shot at them from behind the cover of the trees, which meant he'd seen their faces. More so, he knew Sky was a ranger, and he'd probably gotten an even better look at her before she noticed the body and ran. How much would it take for him to figure out who she was?

Maybe the carabiner meant nothing, and this was a one-off homicide they'd wrap up quickly. But he couldn't shake the nagging thought that Sky might have just put herself in a serial killer's crosshairs.

TWO

Sky scrubbed her face and hands in the bathroom sink, then stared at her reflection. Usually a run left her energized and ready for the day, but this morning she couldn't shake her anxiety over what had happened. Her arms prickled as if a thousand tiny spiders were creeping underneath her skin.

Who was that man and his victim? He'd seen her face. Did he know she hadn't seen his? Would he come after her? Objectively, she should be safe here in the Valley, where there were law enforcement rangers all over the place managing the crowds. But those crowds would make it even harder to catch someone who wanted to blend in.

For a few seconds, she'd thought about leaving, about flying back to Manhattan and crashing at a friend's place until all this blew over. But the night Chris had dumped her instead of proposing had set off a Chernobyl-level catastrophe in her life, and she couldn't face returning to the scene of destruction. Not yet. It was better to stay here and try to carry on like nothing had happened. Like she hadn't failed to be enough for the man she loved.

She pulled her long hair into a ponytail and smoothed down her gray ranger shirt, then headed out of her tent cabin—a wooden frame with canvas walls—to where

Bode waited outside. It was thoughtful of him, escorting her home and then back to work, especially when he had so much to do. He had his back to her as he spun in a slow circle, surveying the seasonal housing. She hadn't paid much attention to his appearance before, in the chaos of the morning, but now she couldn't help noticing his broad shoulders and muscular arms and the way the sunlight glinted off his blond hair. He'd been out climbing when she ran into him, hadn't he?

When he turned and noticed her, she buried all those observations in a box deep in the back of her mind and offered a polite smile. Thankfully, since she wasn't in law enforcement, they wouldn't be working together after her part in this case ended. She had come out here to heal from her breakup with Chris and get over the stress of city life; the last thing she wanted was to tiptoe anywhere near attraction to a new man.

Her bruised and battered heart couldn't take it. Four years she'd invested in that relationship. Four years of working her tail off in an advertising firm, of shopping in the right stores, of mingling with the right crowd, all so she would live up to the expectations of her Wall Street boyfriend with his designer Italian suits.

And what had he done? Invited her out to one of the most expensive restaurants in the city, where she'd fully expected him to propose, only to tell her he'd met someone else. That he didn't think they were right for each other after all.

Never again.

Thankfully, Bode was entirely unaware of the negative memories racing through her brain like Formula 1 cars as they walked back over to the Visitor Center. She led the way to a shared workstation in the back and, with his help, attempted to locate her phone through her online account.

"It says it's offline." She blew out a slow breath. "The most recent location was along the trail."

"Could still be out there, then." He tapped the desk with his fingers. "Cell service is almost nonexistent in that part of the Valley. Why don't you lock it, and we'll check back later? I'll keep an eye out when I go back to the scene."

"Thanks." She logged out, then stood and walked with him back to the large, front counter where she would be spending the day answering visitors' questions. Maps of the park and other printed information covered the surface beneath sheets of glass. Lines of people stood waiting to ask their questions, and restless children ran in circles around their parents' legs. Good. Right now she needed to be busy. "Can you keep me posted on what you find? If you figure out who...?" She let the words trail off.

"Of course." His smile warmed her heart, but she kept her face neutral. He was only doing his job, being kind and thoughtful because of what she'd gone through that morning.

"Thanks, Bode. I mean, Agent Tucker." Heat crept into her cheeks. They were at work, after all. "I really appreciate everything you've done for me today."

"You're welcome. And please, call me Bode. After what we went through, first names are appropriate, don't you think?"

"I guess you're right." She nodded, then waved goodbye. Once he was gone, she turned her focus to the line of visitors waiting for help. The busyness kept her distracted from what Bode and the other law enforcement officers must be doing. Her hands itched to grab her phone to check for updates, but it was lost somewhere in the woods. Most likely he'd either have to call the desk here to give her an update or come in person later. He'd given her his cell number just in case anything came up, but she wouldn't be using it to call him. The thought of seeing the tall ISB agent again was far more appealing than it should be.

Over her lunch break, Sky grabbed a to-go Cobb salad from the snack bar and attempted to track her phone again online. No update. It still appeared offline. By now the battery had probably died. On her day off, she might need to drive out to El Portal to see about replacing it. In the meantime, she'd have to settle for a prepaid phone from the gift shop.

When she returned to the front desk, the line of visitors was still waiting, but something else caught her eye. A bouquet of flowers in a glass vase sat on the back counter—roses, lilies and daisies—all white except for sprays of greenery. She frowned. Where had she seen arrangements like this before?

"What's with the flowers?" she asked Madison, one of her fellow interpretive rangers, as soon as they had a break.

The girl, a college student in her early twenties, pointed at the white envelope nestled among the flowers. "They're for you. A delivery guy dropped them off while you were at lunch."

An uncomfortable jolt rattled through her system. Could they be from Chris? Only a few weeks had passed since he'd broken up with her. Had he changed his mind?

Did she even want him to?

No. Not after the way he'd treated her. She'd never trust him again. Actually, she might never trust any man again, after what he'd done.

Besides, with his penchant for conspicuous spending, he would've sent two dozen long-stem red roses, not this bouquet that looked like it belonged at the end of somebody's coffin. That was it. They looked like memorial service material.

"Who's it from? Your…boyfriend?" The way Madison hesitated suggested she didn't think much of the bouquet either, but she was trying to be polite.

Sky plucked the envelope out of the funeral arrangement. "I don't have a boyfriend." The outside was blank. Her brows pinched together. "How do you know this is for me?"

"Oh, the delivery guy said it was for the ranger with red hair who'd been here earlier. I asked if he meant Ranger Skylar Jansen, and he said, 'Yes.' When I told him you were at lunch, he said it was fine to sign for you. I hope you don't mind."

A chill slithered down her spine. Madison didn't know what had happened earlier that morning, and even if she did, there was no reason to assume this was related. Maybe there was a mix-up, and it wasn't even for her.

She ran a finger beneath the flap, then pulled out a white card. "*With Sympathy*" was printed in metallic gold cursive on the front. The hairs on her arms stood up.

Inside, a message had been handwritten in bubbly print, very much at odds with what the words meant:

Nice meeting you this morning. – J

"Who's it from?" Madison asked, then turned away to help a visitor who'd walked up to the counter.

Her legs wobbled, and she clutched the countertop so hard her knuckles ached. *Jeremy.* She needed to tell Bode about this, now.

Madison glanced back at her, worry creasing her forehead. "Are you all right? Is it a stalker or something?"

No, she wasn't all right. Her chest was so tight she could scarcely draw breath. Black dots swam at the edges of her vision. "I just…need a minute."

She pressed the card against her stomach and slipped down the hall into the administrative area. An office door opened, and she nearly jumped out of her skin as another employee walked out. Maybe the anxiety was justified, but it sure wasn't helpful.

You're safe, she told herself over and over, trying to talk her body out of its fight-or-flight response. Right now, there was no immediate threat. She needed to calm down and call Bode. And since she hadn't activated her prepaid phone yet, she'd have to use a landline. Bode would know what to do. Maybe this card would even help them catch the killer, somehow, although the words had probably been written by someone at the florist's shop.

She kept going down the hall, searching for an empty office to slip inside. Sure, there were plenty of phones—any one of these people would gladly let her make a call, especially if she explained why. But she felt vulnerable enough already. All she wanted was to hide until Bode could get here.

The office at the end was dark. She glanced at the nameplate as she stepped inside—Annetta Lawrence, her supervisor. Annetta must've left early or gone to a meeting. She wouldn't mind if Sky used her phone, and no one would overhear her down here at the end of the hall.

After flipping on the light, she walked over to Annetta's desk and pulled the note with Bode's number out of her pocket. She'd lifted the handset when the room's lights suddenly cut out. A dark figure stood in the open doorway, framed by the light in the hallway. The man from this morning?

Sky's mouth opened, but she couldn't breathe enough to force out any words. She watched in mute horror as the man dropped something on the ground. Glass shattered. He pulled the door shut, and the room filled with the caustic smell of bleach, burning her sinuses and making her eyes water. Light from the hall came in through the door's window, revealing a growing puddle of liquid darkening the carpet.

She needed to get to fresh air, *now.* She dropped the handset and dashed for the door. Her boots crunched with each step over the broken glass, and a heavy, sweet smell rose up from the floor beneath her feet. What *was* that?

Her head suddenly felt like a rock stuck to her shoulders, and the room swayed before her eyes. She felt the cool metal of the doorknob beneath her fingers and twisted, but nothing happened.

Why was every thought, every motion, so hard? Like her body had turned into a metal construction machine, and each limb was a heavy excavator arm. Dropping to her knees, she crammed her face near the bottom of the door, but light no longer streamed in beneath it.

"Help." She tried to scream it, but the word came out as a mere breath. There were no windows in this room. And she didn't have the strength to wrestle the door open.

What was this chemical doing to her? Probably leaching the oxygen out of her blood. Until none was left.

She was going to die in here.

The thought gripped her entire being like a giant hand squeezing a stress ball. *Please, God, I don't want to die.* Bode's note crumpled against her fingers. The phone… Could she still get to the phone?

Like a weightlifter lifting a heavy barbell, Skylar forced her uncooperative body up from the ground and away from the cloying, sweet smell forming over the puddle. She staggered across the room before collapsing into Annetta's chair. Blackness cluttered the edges of her vision, and it took all her concentration to reset the switch to get a dial tone again and type in Bode's number. Was she even reading it correctly in this dim light?

The phone dropped from her hand, and the numbers on the note blurred before her eyes. Her head was so, so heavy. She managed the last digit—was it the last?—and then let her body slump forward onto the desk as darkness overtook her.

Bode steered his NPS vehicle into the long line of traffic heading east into the Valley. The dashboard clock showed 3:00 p.m. That left him only a couple of hours to get this evidence packaged for the lab before he'd have to go pick up Harper. He needed to update Sky, too.

There'd been another body, reduced to bones, in the hole where her attacker had been about to bury the woman. From the state of decomposition of the clothing, they'd estimated this other victim had been buried between five and ten years ago. A carabiner had been found resting on the dorsal surface of the skull, right where the individual's nose would've been. When Bode left, a pair of deputies had just arrived from the sheriff's office with a ground-penetrating radar. If they *were* dealing with a serial killer, there might be more remains buried in this area.

A lot more, if the killer had been active for as long as that skeleton had been buried.

Bode gritted his teeth. Although this was the reason he did this job, it was also the part he hated the most. Because even though he might help bring closure and justice for the families by catching the killer—and preventing more deaths—he still had to witness firsthand the depths of human depravity apart from God.

His phone rang, and he grabbed it from its holder on the

dash. The caller ID read "Annetta Lawrence," the supervisor for the seasonal interps. Was she calling about Skylar?

As he braked behind a slowing vehicle, he swiped to take the call. "Agent Tucker here. What's up?"

Silence. He glanced at the phone to see if the call had disconnected, but the timer was still going. Then a thump sounded, as if someone on the other end had dropped something.

"Annetta?"

His heart rate ticked up a notch. Something felt wrong. He was about to hang up and try calling her back when a fire alarm issued from the phone's speaker.

That was it. He was heading over there ASAP. Maybe he was overreacting, but after the day he'd had, he really didn't like the idea of leaving Sky to face whatever was happening by herself.

After flicking on the emergency lights and siren, he pulled his vehicle onto the shoulder to skirt past the long line of visitors' cars. Traffic in this valley was notoriously bad in summer, but with his lights on, he made it into the Visitor Center parking lot a few minutes later.

People were piling out of the exits, families clustering on the sidewalks and rangers directing traffic. No sign of a fire truck yet, but no sign of smoke either. Had it been an accidental alarm pull? Somebody's toddler who wandered off unattended?

He pulled to a stop in one of the designated ranger parking spots and climbed out, scanning the crowds for a redheaded woman in a ranger uniform, but there was no sign of her. The emergency exit near the offices was open, so he jogged in that direction, flagging down another ranger.

"What's going on?"

The ranger, a fresh-faced college student from the look

of her, went wide-eyed at the sight of an ISB agent. "Fire alarm, sir. I'm just making sure the building is evacuated."

Bode waved her on. If he wanted to make sure Sky wasn't still inside, he'd have to check himself.

Bright lights from the alarm system flashed white overhead as he stepped inside the hallway of admin offices. The place appeared empty, all the office doors open—except Annetta's.

He shoved through the door, nearly tripping on something lying on the floor. A towel, which had been tightly wedged beneath the door. Warning bells blared in his mind louder than the fire alarm, especially when a wave of sickly-sweet chloroform hit his face. He coughed, then gulped in a breath of fresh air from the hall before turning back into the room.

His heart stuttered when he saw a flash of red hair scattered across the desk. Holding his breath, he raced over and hoisted her up and over his shoulder in one swoop. She felt as limp as one of Harper's stuffed animals as he dashed back outside. He carried her over to a patch of grass a safe distance from the building, then eased her to the ground. Across the parking lot, a fire truck pulled up outside the front entrance.

Her eyelids fluttered, her long, dark lashes moving against pale cheeks.

"Skylar?" He brushed a loose strand of hair from her forehead. "Sky, you okay?"

She turned toward him, and her gray-green eyes slowly came into focus. "Bode?" Her voice sounded thick, like she was talking around a mouthful of peanut butter.

He smiled, relief barreling into his chest. Maybe a little disproportionate considering he'd only met her that morning, but after what they'd already been through together, he hated to see her in this situation. "Yeah, I'm here. What happened?"

She pushed herself into a sitting position, and he braced a hand behind her back to help her up. "I… I'm not sure. I…" She blinked, then shook her head like she was trying to clear it. "I went into Annetta's office to call you, and someone dropped a glass jar on the floor. With chemicals in it. Then I blacked out."

He frowned. "It smelled like chloroform. Let's get you checked out, and then we'll figure out what happened." He'd need to examine that room and see the security camera footage. But first, Skylar needed medical attention.

Bode stood, flagging down one of the firefighters as she exited the building, then jogged over to meet her. "What's the status?"

"No fire. The alarm appears to have been triggered accidentally. We're about to let everyone back in."

He pointed toward the emergency exit, which was still propped open. "There's a chemical spill in one of the offices that needs to be treated as a crime scene. Don't touch anything in there."

"I'll tell the others." She headed back toward the front.

Bode pulled out his phone as he walked back to Sky. A quick call to Chief Kleinman would set the crime scene investigation in motion until Bode could get back.

After hanging up, he helped Sky to her feet. She leaned on his arm as he guided her over to his SUV and into the front passenger seat. They drove the short distance to the Valley's medical center, where he checked her into the emergency clinic.

"I'm going back to the Visitor Center to help with the crime scene. I've told the staff here to call me when you're cleared, and I'll come get you."

"No, I can walk. I don't want to put you to all this trouble." A shadow passed across her features. "Actually, I forgot—there's something else you need to see at the Visitor Center."

"See? All the more reason to let me pick you up." After what had just happened, he'd need to talk with the sheriff's office about assigning a patrol officer to watch her place overnight. "What is it?"

Her throat bobbed, and the haunted look returned to her eyes. "He sent me flowers."

Bode frowned. "Who?"

She glanced around, as if someone in the waiting room might be listening. "The killer. I was going back to call you when he shut me in with the chemicals. It was a white bouquet. You have to see the note. I must've dropped it in Annetta's office."

Heat flamed in his chest at the man's brazenness and the way he'd threatened Skylar. "Then we should have him on our video feed. I'll be back for you soon, okay?"

After leaving her in the care of a nurse, Bode hustled back over to the Visitor Center. The interior was once again full of people, but his gaze settled almost immediately on the vase of flowers sitting on the counter behind the front desk. Just as Sky had said. They'd need to add that to their collection of evidence. He gave the rangers strict instructions not to touch it, then strode down the hall back to Annetta's office. A team was already at work inside the small space, taking samples and bagging anything that might be useful. Masks covered their faces, and the door to the outside was propped open to allow better ventilation.

"What've you got?" Bode asked from the doorway.

A dark-haired man glanced up from the floor, where he was swabbing samples of the spilled chemicals that had eroded patches of the carpet to reveal the concrete beneath.

Bode recognized him immediately as Jace Rivera, one of his fellow ISB agents along with Graham Burke and Special-Agent-in-Charge Reese Henlow.

"Jace, glad you could join the party. Henlow said you were busy."

Even though the mask hid his smile, Bode could see it in the crinkles around his eyes. "I had a little break. Wouldn't want to miss out on this." He gestured down at the floor. "Bleach and isopropanol, I'm guessing. Makes chloroform and hydrochloric acid, which is why the carpet is so degraded."

Neither of which was great for humans. Bode nodded grimly, then grabbed a pair of nitrile gloves from one of the collections kits. Stepping carefully around Jace, he scanned the room for any sign of the note Sky had mentioned. There—a cream-colored square lay on the floor beneath Annetta's chair. He stooped to pick it up, then frowned as he read the message. No wonder she'd rushed to call him. She must've been terrified.

He sealed the card inside a collections bag. "Let's get this stuff back to the evidence lab." After requesting the video footage from the camera feeds, he went back to the front to get the flower vase.

"Those were for Skylar Jansen," one of the rangers said as he picked it up.

"I heard. Did you see who delivered it?"

The girl shook her head. "Just some delivery guy. He had a hat pulled low, and I didn't pay attention."

Maybe they'd get more off the security camera footage. "I need to take them, as they might be related to—" he broke off, not sure what Sky had told her "—to the fire alarm being triggered." Best to leave it at that, rather than start more gossip circulating.

Ten minutes later, he pulled up near the back section of park headquarters, where the ISB office and their small crime lab were housed. They didn't have much in the way of technology, but he could at least begin a preliminary analysis and decide what needed to be shipped to the county sheriff's larger lab. He'd barely gotten all the evidence carried in from his vehicle when his phone rang. The call was from the medical center, letting him know Sky had been cleared to leave.

He groaned as he noticed the time—nearly 5:00 p.m. He'd have to pick up Harper right after going to the medical center. Hopefully Sky wouldn't mind.

She was waiting for him inside the lobby when he arrived. It was hard to miss the smile that lit up her face when she recognized him, but she tucked it away almost as soon as it appeared. He didn't know much about her—why she'd moved here or what she'd left behind—but honestly, things were probably better this way. After what he'd gone through with Isla, relationships would never be on the menu again—and he'd do everything in his power to protect Harper from experiencing that kind of loss a second time. After that smile Sky had let slip out, he didn't want to accidentally advertise that he was available. He *wasn't.*

Then again, maybe she was just happy to see a safe, friendly face.

"How are you?" he asked.

She shrugged. "Well enough to break out of here. My throat is a little scratchy and my head still hurts, but the doctor said that might linger a few days. What did you find?"

"The flowers, for starters. And the creepy note. I'm sorry you had to read that." Most likely it had come directly from a florist, so there wouldn't be much in the way of clues, but anything helped. He walked with her out through the sliding doors and into the parking lot, pointing at his personal vehicle, which he'd driven instead of his park SUV. "I have to pick up my daughter from day care. Do you mind tagging along?"

"Oh. Not at all." She blinked, as if absorbing this new information about him. Suddenly he felt the need to explain.

"My wife passed away a couple of years ago, and now it's just me and Harper. They have an employee day care out in El Portal near my home too, but I prefer having her here, close by work, since my hours can get long."

He avoided her gaze as they climbed into the car and he turned on the engine. Sky had never asked for his life story; he wasn't sure why he'd felt like she needed to know.

"I'm sorry," she said, as they pulled out of the lot. "That must've been so hard for you."

His throat grew thick, and he swallowed. *Get a grip, Tucker.* It had been more than two and a half years. He needed to move beyond this and carry on with his life. "Thanks."

They pulled up in front of the gaily painted employee day care center with one minute to spare. The receptionist waved them in. "Well, look at you, all on time."

Heat crept up his neck, and he glanced at Sky. "I've been late a few times." *That* was the understatement of the century. He did his best, especially on early start days when he dropped Harper off before breakfast, but there was only so much he could control with his job. His sister, who lived down in Fresno, had offered more than once to take Harper for him until she reached school age. But the thought of giving up his little girl, even temporarily, hurt too much to consider. Maybe one day his sister would understand that and let it go.

Harper was sitting at a table coloring with markers when he and Sky reached her classroom. Her head was bent over her work, her golden curls cascading over her shoulders. She'd gotten her hair color from them both, but the hazel eyes that sparkled when she looked up came from Isla. "Daddy!" she squealed, then jumped out of her chair and ran to him.

His heart swelled as he stooped and caught her in a bear hug. Yet again, he felt unspoken words of gratitude drifting up to his Heavenly Father. Such a precious gift, his daughter. He glanced at Sky to see her smiling.

"This is Harper." He scooped up the little girl. "Harper, this is Miss Skylar. She's a friend of mine from work." Maybe "friend" was a stretch, since they'd only met that morning. Sky offered his daughter a big, friendly grin.

"Hi, Harper. It's so nice to meet you!"

Harper smiled shyly, pressing her face against his chest. But when he moved to collect her backpack, she reached her chubby hands for the ranger. Sky laughed, a soft, tinkling sound that made him think of Christmas lights and happier times, and opened her arms.

"Here, I can take her." When Sky held out her hands, his daughter let him pass her over without complaint. She dropped her head onto Sky's shoulder, letting out a loud yawn. "Someone is sleepy. I am too, Harper."

"I'm sure you are. It's been quite a day." He grabbed Harper's princess backpack and thanked her teacher, then held the door open for them. His daughter looked perfectly content in Sky's arms, her fingers twirling the long ends of Sky's red hair.

He opened the rear car door, then settled Harper into her car seat. After he and Skylar climbed into the front, he turned to her. "She likes you. She's not usually around a lot of adults other than me, her teachers or my sister, but I can tell she feels safe with you."

"She's a sweet little girl. I don't get to—"

His phone rang, interrupting her words. He glanced at the number, then picked it up. "The chief ranger." He apologized, then accepted the call.

"Agent Tucker here."

"You'd better get back here," Kleinman said grimly. "And bring Ranger Jansen with you. She'll want to hear this."

His gaze locked with Skylar's. From the expression on her face, she'd heard every word. Doubtless she was wondering the same thing: What *worse* news were they about to find out?

THREE

Sky couldn't help but feel sorry for sweet little Harper as Bode pulled her from her car seat in the lot at park headquarters.

"I'm sorry, sweetheart, I know you're tired."

The little girl had three fingers stuffed into her mouth, but she pulled them free at his words. "And hungy. Me want fishies."

"Fishies?" Sky's forehead crinkled. It had been years since she'd been around a small child. Most of her friends in Manhattan were single, and her younger sister, Addie, didn't have kids yet.

"Cheddar fish crackers." Bode winced. "She doesn't always have the healthiest diet. Do you mind grabbing her backpack? There should be a snack in there."

Sky reached past him and tugged the blue princess bag out of the back seat. "Maybe we can find you some dinner too, Harper." Her own stomach growled at the thought, and her cheeks warmed as Bode laughed. He had a nice laugh, natural and inviting. Her ex had always sounded like he was laughing at her, not with her.

Their mini parade finally made it inside to Roger Kleinman's office. Maybe while they were here, she could ask about the police assigning a patrol officer to watch over her tent cabin tonight. The thought of that man lurking outside, with nothing but canvas to keep him out, sent shivers up her spine.

Bode knocked on the door, and Chief Kleinman called for them to enter. An older woman sat inside across from him, maybe in her mid-forties, dressed in a police officer's uniform. They both stood as Bode and Sky entered.

"This is Deputy Cherise Morgan." The chief ranger made the introductions. "She's here to fill you in on what they found with the GPR."

At her quizzical expression, Bode leaned closer. "Ground-penetrating radar," he explained. "It's used to search for remains beneath the surface." When Chief Kleinman's gaze landed on Harper, Bode carried her over to a chair in the corner. "How about a show and a snack?"

The little girl clapped, and soon soft crunching accompanied the sounds of cartoon characters in the background. After he and Sky took seats near the deputy, he turned back to Harper, gazing affectionately at his daughter. What had happened to Harper's mother? Managing a young child all alone had to be difficult for him, especially with this job. And then adding the grief of losing a spouse? How had he done it?

After a moment, he turned his attention back to the desk, and they drew in close to speak in low voices. Chief Kleinman swiveled his computer monitor toward them, then nodded at the deputy.

Cherise pointed to the screen as several mostly black images popped open. In each image, odd little colored-and-gray horizontal bands sat stacked beneath what appeared to be a line demarcating surface level. Sky squinted, struggling to make out what any of it meant.

"This is ground level," Cherise confirmed what Sky

had thought. "And these bands you see in white or different colors are showing things buried beneath the surface."

"It works by shooting an electromagnetic wave into the ground, which bounces back up when it comes in contact with something," Bode added.

"Right." Cherise nodded. "We divide the area into a grid and then walk the GPR unit in lines to cover the entire area. Each line produces one of these images. For example, this one shows you the section with the hole." She pointed at a stack of gray bands. "Here's the other set of remains Agent Tucker discovered this morning." She nodded at Chief Kleinman, who clicked open a new image. "This is another line of data taken about five feet away from the previous set."

Skylar's mouth formed into an O as her eyes landed on the stack of gray bands near one edge of the image. "Is that…?"

"Another body." Bode dragged a hand over his face. "It's definitely not a buried pipeline out there. What's the orientation of this image?"

Cherise pointed at the bands. "This end is on the side near the river. But this is the part you need to see." She moved her finger to hover over a narrow set of black-and-white bands, curved into a distinctive upside-down V shape.

Bode's forehead furrowed. "That's metal."

"We confirmed it with a metal detector," the deputy added.

Then he let out a slow breath, turning toward Sky. She could almost *see* the wheels cranking in his mind, but she still didn't know what it meant. "Your father had a prosthetic leg, didn't he?"

Sky's breath crystallized in her chest. Could it be him? After all these years? Slowly, she nodded. "He lost his left leg below the knee in a car accident when I was seven." She pressed a hand to her mouth as the possibilities washed over her. Had her father run into this same killer while out for a walk all those years ago? Or was this some random hunk of metal not related to him at all?

All these years, her family had lived under the shadow of his disappearance. Her mother had shrunk inside herself as the weeks turned into months, then years, with no word of him. Had she ever secretly doubted his faithfulness? Wondered if he had left with that woman, as a witness came forward to claim? Sky's mom had never said as much to Sky, but this—if these were his remains—would put to rest any possible doubt. Mom might finally be able to move on.

"That's the last place he was seen," she added. Bode nodded, his face a mask of compassion. Of course, he would know. Her father's disappearance was one of Yosemite's most famous cold cases. "I want to be there when you dig. Please."

Bode glanced between Sky and the chief ranger, stealing a moment to consider his answer. He couldn't blame her. *He* was dying to know whether those remains belonged to Andy Jansen, and he wasn't even a blood relative. Just a dedicated agent who'd seen this case pinned to the office wall ever since he took the job. And given what had already happened today, keeping Sky close made perfect sense.

The fact he found her attractive—he could be honest with himself—was just something he'd have to deal with. By ignoring it. That was all there was to it.

"It's fine with me," he said to Kleinman. "Agent Henlow probably already told you, but I'll be handling this case for the ISB. Ranger Jansen might have valuable information to add, too."

Kleinman leaned back in his chair, hands propped behind his head, and surveyed Skylar. "I met Andy once, years ago when I spent a summer working in Kings Canyon. You remind me of him. Same love of the outdoors. Same courage." He offered her a kind smile, the type she deserved after the day she'd had. "Assist Agent Tucker as long as you'd like. I'll clear it with Ranger Lawrence."

"Thank you." She blinked rapidly a few times, then glanced at Bode, and he felt the same spark that had passed between them earlier in the day. From the color rising in her cheeks, he wasn't the only one to notice. *Great.* Hopefully she meant to ignore it, too, or things were going to get uncomfortable. "It won't be for long, I promise. I wouldn't want to interfere with your work."

"I appreciate that." Behind him, Harper squealed with laughter over something in her show. Poor kid. He couldn't keep doing this to her, keeping her away from home all day long. And now that he had this new case, even his weekends might end up booked. "I should be getting her home." He turned to the deputy. "Can you spare a patrol officer to stand watch over Ranger Jansen's cabin? After what happened this afternoon, I don't like the idea of leaving her alone."

He knew better than to ask Kleinman. While Yosemite maintained a list of "on call" rangers for nighttime emergencies, the NPS didn't have the funding to pay anyone to stand guard all night.

"Of course," Deputy Morgan said. "I'll call in the request, but it'll take a bit before someone can get out here."

Too bad he hadn't remembered to ask sooner. He glanced at Harper again, curled up in the chair, her blond curls bouncing against her cheeks as she giggled at her show. Orange cracker crumbs dusted the front of her T-shirt.

A gentle touch on his arm pulled his attention back to Sky. "What if we grab some dinner, and then I can hang out with Harper while you catch up on the case? Just until the patrol officer arrives? I can activate the prepaid phone I bought, too."

Yeah, actually, that might be a good plan. He smiled gratefully. "Let's do it. And thanks for the suggestion."

Twenty minutes later, he settled into his desk chair with a chicken Caesar salad and an iced tea. Across the office, Sky and Harper sat inside a small, glass-walled conference room, their meals spread out on the table. Harper had her back to him, but he could see her small hands waving as Sky said something to her. Between the grin lighting Sky's face and loose strands of red hair dancing against her cheeks, she looked pretty.

Like a distraction he shouldn't be noticing.

He pulled his attention back to his computer and clicked through to the newest files uploaded to his team's shared drive. It was the security camera footage for the front room and the back hallway of the Visitor Center, exactly what he needed. He stabbed a bite of chicken and lettuce, then chewed slowly as he opened the first file and played through at quadruple speed. When the vase of white flowers appeared in the frame, he clicked pause, then played it through in slow motion.

The delivery man wore a dark shirt and pants, along with a ball cap on his head. But somehow he managed to carry the flowers so that they were always blocking his face, almost as if he knew right where the camera was located. Could *this* man be Sky's assailant? But why would he risk delivering those in person, when he could've hired any flower company? Unless he wanted to verify her identity?

The thought sent a surge of fear through his limbs. They'd already uncovered multiple bodies. If the man knew her name, where she worked, what she looked like… Bode rolled his shoulders. Worrying wasn't going to help anybody. Instead, he needed to focus on what he could control—catching the culprit.

Like the ranger had said, the man deposited the vase on the counter, then ducked his head low as he waited for her signature on the receipt. He turned around, walking though the throng of visitors back toward the door. Never once giving up a clear shot of his face.

The plastic fork in Bode's hand snapped, and he released the fist he'd unconsciously made. *Deep breaths.* They'd find this guy. Anyone cocky enough to waltz right into the Visitor Center and commit a crime would make a mistake sooner or later.

Bode took a swig of iced tea, then stuffed in more food, barely tasting it, as he watched Sky appear on the screen. She examined the flowers and picked something out from between them—the envelope with the note he'd found in Annetta's office.

He skipped ahead, watching in double time as she read the note and headed out of the camera's field of vision. After noting the time stamp, he pulled up the corresponding feed for the office hallway.

She appeared again on screen, heading down the hall, glancing at the doors as she passed. Her back was toward the camera as she stepped into the last room on the left—Annetta's. Then someone else stepped into view, and Bode nearly choked on a crouton.

It was the same man. The height, the build, the dark

clothes and ball cap—they were all the same as the flower delivery guy, following Sky down the hall as if he'd been watching her the whole time. Yet again, he kept his face down and tilted away from the camera. Something flashed in his hands—the glass jar of chemicals. He vanished partway into the office, then reappeared, pulling the door shut behind him. After stooping, he stuffed something beneath the door. He lingered outside for a moment and almost looked like he was about to reach for the handle again when he suddenly stiffened, then bolted out the emergency exit as if he'd heard someone coming.

Pushing the door open must've triggered the alarm. Skipping ahead on the feed showed everyone evacuating the building. Bode clicked through the other files and found the camera feed that showed the emergency exit, but there was only a short clip of the man running out, a hand over the bill of his ball cap. He vanished off-frame almost immediately, heading in the direction of the woods at the back of the building.

Bode exhaled a slow breath. The man could be anywhere by now. And there was no doubt he knew exactly who Skylar was. Did he know her relationship to Andy Jansen? And was he the killer or an accomplice of some sort?

Please don't let there be two of them, Lord.

Laughter reached his ears, and he glanced up to see Sky playing some sort of hand-clapping game with Harper. Some of the tension loosened in his chest at the sight of his daughter looking so happy. It had been far too long since she'd enjoyed attention from anyone outside their very limited circle.

His phone rang—the patrol officer had pulled into the lot outside the building. Bode wolfed down the rest of his salad and threw away the trash. He'd need to get into the employee database to look for a trail maintenance worker named "Jeremy," but that could wait until Harper was in bed. And would the man have given his real name? Not likely.

After shutting off his computer, he walked over to the conference room, pausing in the doorway to listen to his daughter's giggles. Sky hadn't noticed him. She was in the middle of singing a song about farm animals and making *cheep-cheep* noises at Harper. He clapped when she finished, and her cheeks tinged pink.

"I didn't see you there. We were just…singing."

Harper spun around in her chair. "Daddy! Chickies say *cheep-cheep*."

He laughed. "Yes, they do, little peanut. Are you all done eating?"

When she nodded, he walked over and helped gather up the trash. "You have a beautiful singing voice," he told Sky. "Much better than my frog croaks. And you have a way with children." He gestured at Harper, who was clapping her hands and singing to herself.

She tucked her chin. "I've missed being around kids. I didn't see them often in my day-to-day life in New York, and my sister is newly married without any of her own yet. Harper is a delight." She glanced at the little girl, then back to him. Something almost wistful flitted across Sky's features, making her eyes shine. They were the most unique color, like the storm-tossed waters of the Pacific under a gray sky.

She cleared her throat, and heat crept up the back of his neck as he realized he'd literally been staring into her eyes. What had come over him? He jerked his attention back to Harper and helped her gather her things.

"The patrol officer is here. Let's get all of us home, okay?"

"Did you find anything on the video footage?" she asked as they headed out of the conference room.

He flicked off the small room's lights and closed the door. "Yes, your delivery guy matches the description you gave of the man this morning, but he never shows his face on camera. He appeared to follow you down the hall."

She took the news as well as could be expected, pressing a hand to her mouth but staying steady on her feet. "Then he knows for sure who I am."

"I'm sorry, but I think he does." Bode longed to offer comfort, to place his hand on her back or embrace her as he'd unintentionally done that morning, but he kept his hands at his sides. He could tell Skylar appreciated the truth, that she didn't want to be coddled. It made him respect her all the more. "We'll find him. As soon as I get Harper in bed, I'll keep doing research from home. See if we can turn up any leads among the trail maintenance team."

"Thanks." She offered him a weak smile as he opened the front door.

Together they found the patrol car. Deputy Walcott, a balding man in his mid-forties with a mustache, introduced himself.

"Keep me posted?" she asked as she climbed into the passenger seat.

"You got it. I'll be in touch first thing about going back to the scene for excavation." He flashed the Post-it note she'd given him earlier with her new cell number.

Holding Harper close, he waved as the patrol car drove off, then bundled the little girl into his vehicle. "Ready to go home, sweetheart?"

"Okay, Daddy. Me want Leepop." She settled back into her car seat, and he tucked her blanket up under her chin, a sad smile stretching his face. Lollipop, or Leepop as Harper called her, was a soft gray elephant Isla had bought when she found out they were having a girl. Each night Harper snuggled the worn stuffed animal like she was holding on to a piece of her mom.

"I know you do. It's been a long day." And it would be longer still for him. Thirty-five minutes to drive home, then getting Harper to bed. *Then* he could turn his attention back to this case, where time was of the essence.

That man had to be caught as soon as possible. Because if Bode didn't catch *him*, he might catch Skylar first.

Sky tried to settle into the patrol car's seat, but she couldn't get her spine to loosen. The chief ranger's news hung over her like a dark cloud, or more like a Category 5 hurricane. The killer knew who she was. *And* where to find her. Her palms grew slick, her breath sticking in her throat at the mere thought, and she forced herself to inhale slowly.

You're safe. She'd been repeating the same words to her frazzled system for hours, but her adrenal glands didn't seem to care about logic anymore. Her lungs had been stuck in the same half-capacity mode the entire day, except for maybe that half hour she'd spent playing with Harper. The sweet little girl was the best kind of stress release Sky had ever experienced.

Okay, maybe being around Harper's dad made Sky feel more relaxed, too. And safe. Not only was Bode Tucker good-looking, but he also gave off an air of confidence and strength that immediately imparted a sense of security. As if nothing bad could happen to her when he was there.

She shook off the silly thought. Sure, she could tell Bode

was a good and honest man, but she'd only met him that morning. Entertaining ideas about him beyond law enforcement help on this case was out of the question. Besides, she'd learned her lesson with Chris. Just because her ex was a completely different person than Bode—high-strung instead of laid-back, overachieving, consumed with appearances—didn't mean she ever wanted to walk down that road again. *No thanks.* One broken heart was enough. She'd just have to content herself with the protection of kind, capable Deputy... What was his name? She stole a glance at his name tag as he stopped the car in front of her cabin.

"Thank you, Deputy Walcott. I appreciate it."

He tipped his hat, then climbed out when she did. "Happy to help, ma'am. Let me escort you to the door, then I'll take a walk around the premises. And I'll be parked right out here all night long, so you just give me a holler if anything alarms you."

Her chest eased a fraction as she walked with the deputy up to her front door. If that man—Jeremy, as he'd identified himself—was waiting inside, he wouldn't get the jump on her this time. She unlocked the front door and swung it open, then flipped on the lights. The small interior looked exactly the same as she'd left it. Two twin beds, a wooden chair and metal racks for storage on either side of the door. Most seasonal employees ended up with roommates, but she'd been fortunate enough to have the tiny place to herself. Though right now, it might be nice not to be alone.

Deputy Walcott checked under the beds, then left to walk around the exterior. When she'd gathered up her toiletries to use the shared bathhouse, he offered to walk her the short distance.

"That's all right." She pointed to the nearby wood-sided

building. "You'll be able to see it from here. I should only be twenty minutes or so."

He was sitting in the patrol car by the time she returned, wet hair wrapped up in a towel and dressed in her most comfortable flannel pajamas to ward off the evening mountain chill. Sky made sure to lock the door behind her, then fell backward onto the rickety twin bed. She tried to pray, but the words jammed up in her throat. An image of her dad's face shone in her mind—his brown hair and that wide grin as he teased her about her youthful fear of spiders. Tears pricked her eyes. *Was* it her dad in that grave? And if so, what happened?

Had it been this man, Jeremy, who killed him? Why?

She sat up, swiping at her eyes and reaching into her pack. Dad had loved reading the Bible. She found hers, then flipped it open to the spot where she'd left off. Too many days ago.

Highlighted words from Psalm 121 caught her eye: *The Lord shall preserve thee from all evil: he shall preserve thy soul. The Lord shall preserve thy going out and thy coming in from this time forth, and even for evermore.*

Her breathing calmed as she prayed the words back to God, thanking Him for His promises. Even if her mortal body was in danger, as it had been more than once that day, her soul was safe in His hands. *Thank You, Lord.*

By the time she set her Bible aside and flipped off her light, she felt better. She'd prayed over her situation, over her fears, over what they might find tomorrow. And over Bode and his sweet little daughter.

Her fear didn't vanish, but she did feel better as a sense of God's peace and presence filled her. She fell asleep to the Valley's soothing nighttime sounds, gently hooting owls and the intermittent buzzes and clicks of the insects.

Several hours passed, but she felt like she'd just dozed off when another sound sliced through her sleep and roused her. It was raspy, almost like a saw or something rubbing against fabric. What insect made a noise like that? She lay in her bed listening, half-asleep still, until the sound stopped. Her heart pounded so hard it felt like it was trying to escape her ribs. A breeze rustled her covers, coming in through the screened ventilation window near the apex of the ceiling.

Or wait… Every cell in her body froze. That breeze had come from lower down and close by. The front door was still locked, so where—

The chair she used as a night table shifted sideways as a dark shape climbed into her cabin through a hole in the canvas. She opened her mouth to scream, willing *some* kind of sound to come out—anything to alert the deputy—but a damp rag clamped over her face. Sweet and heavy. Overwhelming. The same as the chloroform she'd inhaled earlier.

Her lungs protested. She tried to cough, tried to thrash for the hand smothering her with the nasty chemical, to fight, but her body felt so very tired. Her limbs refused to move.

Then everything went black.

FOUR

A yawn slipped out as Bode opened his laptop and tapped in the access pin. He eyed the refrigerator with its cold soda cans longingly, but guzzling caffeinated beverages at this hour would ensure a restless night and little sleep. Getting Harper settled for the night had taken longer than he'd wanted, though he could hardly blame her for wanting extra stories and snuggles. She'd fallen asleep in the car on the way home, then gotten a second wind when he carried her inside. With how little time they'd had together lately, it was only natural she'd want to be with him.

He dragged a hand through his hair, fending off the twinge of guilt. Single parenting wasn't for the faint of heart. The familiar thought of *God, why did You let this happen* started to take raw shape in his mind, but he shook his head. He missed Isla, missed her presence, but he knew where she was. Knew she wouldn't want him living in the past. Besides, negative thinking didn't help. It *had* happened, and now he needed to do his best and trust God to take care of the rest. Maybe he and the Lord didn't see eye to eye on His plans, but Bode had no choice other than to go along with them.

Right now, what mattered was figuring out who had attacked Skylar. He opened his internet browser and pulled up access to the park employee database. Based on the victims they'd found, the killer would've had access to that section of the park on multiple occasions over the past several years. Most likely, he'd be someone who either lived in the area or had returned to work in Yosemite for several seasons. He'd start with the obvious—anyone named Jeremy who worked on the trails or in the area—though he doubted the man had given his real name.

A half hour of searching the database produced a couple of potential suspects. A Jeremy Martins who worked trail maintenance, though this season appeared to be only his second, and his photograph made him look larger-framed than the man on the video feed. There was a Jeremy Harding who'd worked for several seasons. His picture on file didn't look like a promising match either, but it was hard to tell from a headshot. He clicked through to another database for seasonal food service employees and found a Jeremy Kramer. Although it was the man's first season with Aramark, the park's contracted concessionaire, he'd been previously employed at a hotel in El Portal. No photograph was on record.

Bode jotted down the names and contact information on a sheet of paper, trying to ignore the sense of frustration churning in his gut. There were thousands of people who worked in and around Yosemite, and many of them were seasonal, switching jobs and moving from year to year. He could hardly go around tracking down every five-foot-ten man in a hundred-mile radius.

But they had to start somewhere. Hopefully they'd get reports soon on the evidence he'd shipped off. Anything to help narrow down the list. Exhaustion coursed through his body in waves, and he rubbed bleary eyes before pulling up NamUs, the national missing persons database. A few minutes later, he had a list of all reports for the area dating back decades. Andy Jansen's name caught his eye immediately. The newest victim, the one the killer had been in the act of burying, most likely wouldn't be listed yet. He'd have to ask the sheriff's office for their most recent list. For now he'd save this file and his potential suspect list to his work server. It wasn't much, but it was a start.

Tomorrow he'd start researching these suspects to see if any of them matched the killer's height and build and determine if they could've been in the area at the right time. And he'd accompany Skylar back to the crime scene to finish digging up the remains. Weariness—and dread at what they might find—wrapped around him as he dragged himself to bed.

The alarm went off what felt like minutes later, and he forced himself through the morning ritual of getting ready. Harper whined and fought as he flipped on her bedroom light, and even *he* knew his attempts to sound upbeat were a dismal failure.

By the time she broke down into sobs, he held her close and pressed a kiss to her soft hair. "I'm so sorry, peanut, but we have to get up for school. Don't you want to see your teachers?"

"No!" Her lower lip stuck out in a pout, and her watery hazel eyes threatened to melt him. "Me want seep! And Leepop." She squeezed the little elephant against her cheek.

"I hear you, sweet pea. I want to sleep, too. But Daddy has to go to work. Remember Miss Skylar? She needs my help, and she's counting on me."

At Sky's name, the little girl brightened. "See Miss Skylar."

He wanted to see Miss Skylar, too, if he was being honest. But only because he wanted to make sure she was safe.

"How about we call her on the way into school? I'll put her on speaker so you can talk as well."

"Okay, Daddy." Her sniffles subsided, and she allowed him to help her get ready.

When they'd eaten a quick breakfast and loaded into the car, he pulled out his cell and clicked through to the number for Sky's pay-as-you-go phone. "Let's call Miss Skylar now."

The phone rang once. Twice. Three times. Adrenaline fired through his veins. Why wasn't she answering? Was she away from her phone in the shower? Or had she muted it?

Finally he cut off the call. She hadn't set up the voice mail yet, so he couldn't leave a message.

"Me wanna talk to Miss Skylar!" Harper yelled from the back seat. "Now!"

"Harper, that's not how we talk to each other. No yelling." He tried to keep his tone calm despite the fear crowding his insides. "Miss Skylar didn't answer."

The traffic was already building on the road as he approached the park's entrance gate. He slowed down, steering into the employees' lane and waving at the ranger on duty, and tapped through to Deputy Walcott's phone. Thankfully the deputy answered after the first ring.

"Hey, this is Special Agent Bode Tucker. I tried calling Ranger Jansen, but she didn't pick up. Do you have a 10-20 on her?"

"Morning, Agent Tucker," the deputy replied. He sounded awake enough—always a good sign when one had an all-night patrol. "She hasn't come out of the cabin yet this morning. Want me to check on her?"

He glanced at the clock. It was still early, 7:15 a.m. Maybe she was merely sleeping in after a rough day yesterday. But his gut thought otherwise. He didn't know Sky well, but she didn't seem like the type who'd be sleeping in on a day when they might be excavating her father's remains. "Yeah, maybe you should. I'll be over there in fifteen, as soon as I drop my daughter off."

Yet again he thanked the Lord that the day care center opened as early as it did, even though he might never shake the guilt he felt dropping Harper off every morning. He pulled into the lot and hustled her out of the car.

"Me wanna see Miss Skylar," she whined as he grabbed her backpack. Her attachment to Sky should be setting off alarms, but right now nothing could compete with his own growing sense of worry.

"I will tell her that as soon as I see her." He nearly dropped the backpack as he struggled to pull the door open. Thankfully, Harper perked up as soon as she was in her classroom, where her teacher guided her over to a table set up with play dough.

He blinked a few times, pressing a hand to his heart, then mouthed, "Thank you," to the teacher. When would life slow down enough that he could truly spend the time with Harper that she deserved?

His phone rang as he climbed back into the car. "Tucker here."

"Bode, it's Jace. We just got an anonymous call to the tip line. I think it might be from your perp."

He steered out of the lot and up the road deeper into the Valley, heading for the seasonal employee housing. "Why? What did he say?"

"The voice is probably AI, but the message is a set of coordinates. Lat and long."

Bode frowned. "Where?"

"Looks to be the location of the crime scene, though I don't know why he'd call to give you that again."

Yeah, that was odd. “Okay. Thanks, Jace.”

He hung up and pulled to a stop behind the deputy’s cruiser, parked in front of a tent cabin. As he climbed out of the car, the deputy appeared from behind the cabin. The man’s expression did nothing to calm the fear gnawing at Bode’s gut.

“Deputy?” Bode walked over to the police car. “Where is she?”

The man cleared his throat, then shook his head. “Someone cut a hole in the canvas at the back of the tent. It wasn’t there on my last perimeter check at 4:30 a.m.”

A pit ripped open in his stomach as Bode dashed around the back. Sure enough, the canvas flapped gently in the breeze where a three-foot gash had been slashed through it. Even though he knew it was pointless, he still peered inside—as if he’d find her sitting on the edge of her bed. But the small space was empty. A nearby chair had been knocked over, scattering papers and upsetting what looked like a small leather-covered Bible. A spurt of warmth cut through the cold fear licking his insides. Was faith something they had in common? *Please, Lord, be with Sky.*

His gaze locked with the deputy. “Did you fall asleep?” He hadn’t meant it to come out so bluntly, so accusatory, but Skylar was *gone*. Possibly for hours, given that it was 7:30 a.m. now.

“No, I did not.” The man stiffened, shaking his head. “Not with someone’s safety on the line.”

Bode’s chest deflated. “Of course, I’m sorry.” Trees lined the area behind the cabin only a few feet away, their limbs stretching high overhead. “He probably snuck up through the woods. We need to process the scene in case he left evidence. And we need to find her.” He rammed a hand through his hair. How could the day feel so long when it had only just begun?

Walcott turned away and started rattling off information into the radio attached to his shoulder. After tugging his phone out of his pocket, Bode put in a call to alert the park's network of rangers to Sky's disappearance. He had just ended the call when another one came through, from Jace again.

"Tucker here. What's up?" Bode asked.

"I heard your APB for Skylar." His voice sounded grim. "And I found a second message on the tip line. It says, 'Time is running out.'"

Bode swallowed. "He's playing a game with us. Maybe he took her to those coordinates, back to the crime scene."

"But why? When we already know what's there?"

"I don't know, but I'm about to find out." He made eye contact with the deputy as he spoke. "Deputy Walcott will monitor the scene at the cabin until our people can get here. Tell Kleinman I'm on my way to the clearing and to send backup."

"You got it."

Bode clicked off the call, then exchanged a nod with Walcott before striding to his car. His gun in its holster, along with a two-way radio—when he remembered to take one—sat locked in the center console, the same place he kept it every time he drove. *Please, Lord, let me not need it. And let Skylar be okay.*

Gripping the wheel, he turned the car around and left the housing area, heading for the road that would take him toward the clearing.

And maybe one step deeper into a killer's twisted game.

Skylar's eyes flicked open to total darkness. Something hard dug into her sternum, and her body was completely immobilized. She lifted her head, thunking her forehead against something solid mere inches from her face. Dull pain throbbed behind her temples, and hazy memories lurched through her mind. A man had broken into her tent cabin. He'd slapped something wet over her mouth—nasty chemicals that knocked her out. That explained the headache.

But where was she? And why couldn't she move?

Her heart rate picked up as she tried to shift her body again. Every inch of her was pinned down except her head, and when she turned it from side to side, the back of her head grated against what felt like—

Dirt. Had she been…buried alive?

Panic ripped through her system, freezing her breath in her chest. What was over her face? She leaned her head, tapping her forehead gently against the sides and the top. It felt cold and smooth against her skin, like plastic. Something to trap a little air, so she didn't suffocate immediately.

But why? So she'd suffer slowly? Drown in this wave of fear that clutched her throat and made her heart race like it might explode?

Her breath came faster, in little huffs, and she pinched her eyes shut, trying to calm her breathing. In through her nose, out through her mouth. *One. Two. Three.* How much oxygen did she have? Or was it the carbon dioxide she exhaled with each breath that would poison her first?

She clamped her mouth shut as her chest tightened like a boa constrictor had found her. Stars swam in her vision, little pinpricks of light blinking against the black.

Please, God, don't let me go this way. He'd helped her before, through Bode, when the killer chased her. He could help her again.

A slow breath siphoned out from between her lips, and

the stars receded. Panicking would not help. But what would?

She grunted, straining against the weight of dirt to move her hands or her feet, then stopped. *Bad idea, Sky.* All she was doing was filling her air space faster with carbon dioxide. It would be smarter to conserve her energy and slow her breathing to exhale as little as possible.

Had the deputy discovered she was missing yet? Was Bode searching for her? Here, in the pitch dark, she had no clue what time it was. Maybe it was still the middle of the night, and no one would realize she was gone for hours yet. Until it was too late.

Her pulse throbbed again, and she begged her body to calm down. Words from Psalm 23 floated through her mind and she latched on to them, saying them over and over: *The Lord is my shepherd; I shall not want. He maketh me to lie down in green pastures: he leadeth me beside the still waters. He restoreth my soul.*

If she lay very still, maybe she could start with her fingers. Find a way to wiggle them and unearth herself. Maybe she wasn't that deep or the soil wasn't as packed as it felt.

Stars flickered on the edges of her vision again, but this time slowing her breathing didn't help. How could she be running out of time already? *Please, Lord!*

She focused on her hands, threading every bit of willpower into moving her fingers. When her left pinkie twitched, hope jolted through her system. At the same moment, she realized there was thumping coming from somewhere above her. Footsteps?

Her first instinct was to scream, but she kept her mouth shut. It wouldn't do any good if they found her after she'd gassed herself to death. Instead, she kept working on the soil with her left hand, wiggling it as the sounds increased overhead. Was someone digging?

Hope and prayers mingled unspoken in her chest, even as the stars blinked brighter in her vision. Her head felt heavy, as if her thoughts were dissolving into fog. Still, she forced her fingers to move. The soil was definitely loosening. With a monumental effort, she bent her arm at the elbow, thrusting her hand up.

A cry sounded somewhere above her, but her hand had grown too heavy to keep moving. Suddenly warm fingers grasped hers. She squeezed back, taking in tiny breaths, praying she could hold out.

Then natural daylight hit her eyes through dusty plastic moments before someone ripped it away. Glorious fresh oxygen hit her face, and she sucked in great gasps, choking and blinking against the dirt falling in her eyes.

"Skylar!" Bode tossed something aside and wrapped a hand beneath her head, helping tug her up until she was sitting.

She swiped dirt away from her face, then looked around. She was sitting with her head barely at ground level, two feet down in a human-sized hole. A plastic storage bin sat off to one side, and Bode crouched next to her. "You found me."

When her gaze met his, he reached down for her. "Come here, let's get you out of there."

She lifted her arms, and he gripped his hands around them, hoisting her to her feet. When she stumbled stepping out of the hole, he caught her in an unexpected embrace.

"Take it easy." His arms wrapped around her in warmth so comforting it stole her breath.

She nodded a little too vigorously, then pushed back as he released her and busied herself brushing dirt off her clothes. Pajamas, actually—the lounge pants and T-shirt she'd worn to bed. Heat singed her cheeks until her hands brushed against something cold and hard clipped to the bottom of her shirt.

"What's that?" He pointed down at the object.

She lifted the hem to reveal a purple metal carabiner. A piece of paper had been punched through one end. She unhooked it and held it up, her gaze meeting Bode's. A frown creased his brow, and the look in his eyes was far more unsettling than what she wanted to see.

The paper crinkled as she unhooked it from the metal and held it out. Words had been scrawled across an otherwise blank sheet: *Like father, like daughter.*

"Here, let me bag that," Bode said grimly. He pulled a plastic sandwich baggie from his utility belt and held it open. She dropped both the note and carabiner inside, then glanced around. They were back in the same clearing where she'd found the man digging. Was it only yesterday? The new hole where he'd buried her had been dug a few feet over from the first. Where had that magnetic imaging found the metal? Was her father buried near here, too? Ice water washed through her veins, but she gritted her teeth. If Dad's remains were here, she'd find them. And then they'd see that his killer was brought to justice.

A gentle hand on her arm snapped her attention back to Bode. "Let's get you back to the clinic and checked out, okay?"

What? *No.* She shook her head. "I'm okay. I just need to get cleaned up, and then I'm staying here while you dig."

His two-way radio crackled to life before he could object. "Tucker, here. Yes, I've got her." He glanced at her, then turned away, as if somehow that would keep her from hearing. "She was buried two feet down in the clearing.

Plastic bin over her face to keep her from suffocating. Yes. Sounds good."

Tears pricked her eyes as he turned back. "You can't shield me from this, Bode. I appreciate that you want to look out for me, but I was abducted and buried *alive*. And more than likely my dad is here, too. I need to know, and *we* need to catch this man before…" A sob hitched her chest, but she covered it with a cough. If he knew what a wreck she was inside, he'd never agree to let her stay.

His hand twitched at his side, but he nodded, keeping his distance. Maybe wanting to reinforce that the embrace earlier had been accidental. "All right. We need to get you moved out of that tent cabin and into something safer. Rangers are on their way here, but we'll come back as soon as we have you taken care of, okay?"

The team of rangers arrived a few minutes later, and she offered a silent prayer of thanks that Bode hadn't waited for backup to start searching for her. Otherwise, she'd be gone by now. The sobering thought clung to her as she and Bode hiked back out to his vehicle.

"How did you know where to find me?" she asked.

"When you didn't answer your phone, I notified the deputy and went to your cabin as soon as I dropped Harper off. We found where the killer cut his way through the canvas. Then he left a couple of calls on the anonymous tip line, giving the geographic coordinates of the clearing. So I assumed that was where he'd taken you."

She frowned. "He did?"

"Yeah. I'm not sure why. It's almost like he wanted us to find you in time."

"Or wanted you to find me just a little too late." The thought chilled her to her bones.

Bode let out a slow breath. "I didn't know he'd buried you until I got there and saw the freshly overturned soil."

"Thank you. You got to me just in time." She went on to explain how she'd awakened in the night to the sound of the canvas being cut and how the killer had abducted her.

His frown deepened as she spoke, and when she finished, he dragged a hand over his face. "It's almost like he's playing some type of sick game. We need to find you safer lodgings."

They climbed into his car and drove back to the tent cabin, where Deputy Walcott apologized profusely. Bode insisted on escorting her to the shared bathhouse, waiting outside as she scrubbed the dirt out of her hair and from behind her ears. She felt like a new person when she emerged twenty minutes later in her ranger uniform.

"As soon as the crime scene is cleared, I'll have someone gather your belongings to relocate to your new housing." He hesitated, as if suddenly aware she might not want someone else touching her things. "If you don't mind?"

She appreciated his thoughtfulness. "That's fine. I just want to get back to the clearing to see what we find." A hard lump formed in her throat, and she swallowed, wrapping her arms across her stomach.

His gaze lingered on her face for a moment. But thankfully, instead of pressing her, he merely pointed to the car. "Let's get moving then, if you're ready."

She stowed her toiletry bag back in the tent cabin. Since the officers on the scene had cleared the storage area, she spent a few minutes packing up her clothing and other loose items from the racks.

After providing an official statement, she and Bode returned to the clearing and ducked beneath the police tape. A half dozen law enforcement rangers and deputies from the Sheriff's Office were already on the scene with shovels and evidence collection toolkits. Chief Kleinman walked up as they approached.

"Ranger Jansen." He offered a kind smile. "I'm glad to see you up and about. How are you feeling?"

She stuffed her hands into her pockets to avoid rubbing her arms. "I'm hanging in there. Ready for answers."

"I'm sure." He turned to Bode. "Agent Tucker, I'll leave you in charge. Sheriff Hart volunteered a deputy to stay on duty overnight if you can't finish before dark. And he's sending a female deputy to room with Ranger Jansen until this is over with."

"Thank you." The crease between Bode's brows relaxed just a little as he turned to her. "Let's get to work."

The sun inched its way high overhead, making sweat bead on Sky's forehead and back as the morning wore into afternoon. Much of it was slow work, and she had little to do besides watch—*and* worry—as the team tagged and recorded surface evidence, then prepared to dig where the ground-penetrating radar had indicated hits.

They took a break in the early afternoon when another ISB agent, whom she recognized from his photograph in the Visitor Center, arrived with white paper sacks. The investigators set aside their equipment, wiping their hands and swigging water from bottles kept in a cooler.

"Is that lunch? You read my mind," Bode announced as the dark-haired agent walked over to them. What was his name? She'd seen his picture just as many times as Bode's, but his name hadn't stuck quite as well. Something about Bode had always caught her eye, and it was more than just the fact he was handsome. In that picture, his eyes had always made her think of him as someone kind and caring. Someone she could trust.

"I figured you were working up an appetite." He handed some of the bags to Bode, then offered his hand. "Jace Rivera. I'm an ISB agent with Bode. And you must be Skylar Jansen. Glad to see this guy found you in time." He nodded toward Bode.

"Me, too." She glanced shyly at Bode. His gaze was on her, studying her with an intensity that made her cheeks flush.

Jace cleared his throat, and Bode abruptly broke eye contact, looking down at the sacks in his hands. He was merely showing his concern, of course. Nothing worth reading into.

"What've we got?" Bode asked.

"Chicken Caesar wraps and ham sandwiches for everyone," Jace announced. "Take your pick."

Sky selected a wrap and a bag of chips before taking a seat on the grass a safe distance away from where they would be digging. Bode joined her, followed by Jace.

"Got anything on the tips we received?"

Jace shook his head at Bode's question. "Nothing to point us to a suspect. Though I did run both messages through an app that confirmed there's a ninety-eight percent chance they were AI generated."

"So someone with at least a bit of tech skills?" Sky was suddenly back in New York, sitting in her cubicle in front of a computer, wrangling images on the screen for a make-or-break advertising campaign. Paper crackled beneath her fingers, and she realized she'd been squishing her wrap.

A puzzled expression flitted across Bode's face. He didn't miss much, did he? "Too bad that's not much to go on. Let's hope we get something on the evidence from Skylar's cabin."

Jace stood. "I've got to get back to my case. Let me know if you need anything else."

"Will do. Thanks for the food, man. Glad you're looking out for me." Bode tapped his chest then pointed at Jace, who waved as he left.

Their easy camaraderie made something twinge beneath Sky's ribs. She'd longed for work relationships like that, but it had been impossible in her marketing firm. Everyone else seemed to view their coworkers as stepping stones to scramble up on their way to the top. How much more pleasant and productive they could've been, if they'd worked together instead of competing.

Tension gripped her lungs again, squeezing her chest until her breath came in shallow bursts. Just the way it had when she'd been trapped beneath that plastic bin, buried alive. At the thought, her heartrate jumped like she was sprinting, foreshadowing a full-on panic attack. *No*, she could not afford to come apart, not now. She'd gotten far too familiar with these awful feelings during her final months in New York. She forced in a slow breath, filling her lungs and holding the air for a second before releasing.

"Hey, you okay?" Bode studied her face. "If you need a break, I can take you back to headquarters."

No way, not when they had a case to solve. She had to pull herself together, shake off this lingering terror clawing at her mind. It had to be the trauma of the past twenty-four hours catching up to her.

"No, I want to be here. Just thinking about my last job." She forced trembling fingers to open her wrap, then took a bite. It tasted good, and the food would help her feel more grounded. More in control. Bode dug into his sandwich but didn't say anything, as if waiting for her to elaborate. Talking about her old life might help get her mind off what had happened that morning too. "I worked for a marketing firm in Manhattan. It was very competitive. High stakes. Lots of backbiting. Not a nice place to be."

"Is that why you moved out here?"

That, and Chris. But Bode didn't need to hear about her dismal love life. "It was time for a change." She inhaled a deep breath of fresh air, glad to find her lungs working for a change. "It's good to be outside again."

"Yeah. And you picked the right park." He rubbed the back of his neck. "Well, other than the whole serial killer thing."

Laughter burbled in her chest at how ridiculous this situation was, as if her emotions couldn't take it anymore and needed *some* outlet. Better to laugh than panic. Maybe eventually, when it was all over, she'd find a silver lining. *Like meeting Bode...?* She swiped away the thought before it could fully form. "Yosemite *is* beautiful. What brought you here?"

He swallowed a bite of sandwich and balled up the paper wrapper. "I'll spare you the long version, but I was a climber out here long before I became a ranger. My boss Reese recruited me into the ISB after working with me on several search-and-rescue operations."

And Harper's mother? She wanted to ask, but the question felt too personal. It was better to keep things light. "That's why you were out climbing yesterday, just for fun?"

"Yep. You see a lot of difficult stuff in this line of work, and it can be hard to process. Climbing helps with that." He gestured to the others who had finished eating. "Looks like we're ready to get started. You all done?"

When she nodded, he climbed to his feet and offered a hand to help her up. His fingers felt warm and strong wrapped around hers, his palms rough from his work.

"You sure you're comfortable being here?" Bode's gentle

tone touched a tender spot buried deep inside, making her almost sad for a moment. Even after years together, Chris had never shown that level of concern. And he certainly wouldn't have wanted an honest answer if anyone else was in earshot. He couldn't risk ruining appearances.

Probably his breaking things off was a blessing, really. She never would've made him happy, and he would've figured it out eventually. But all the logical reasoning in the world wouldn't help the aching sense of failure and loneliness buried deep in her chest.

None of that was Bode's concern, so for his sake, she schooled her face back into a neutral expression. "Absolutely."

The digging went faster than she expected. Maybe faster than she was ready for. It seemed like barely any time had passed before they'd carved a three-foot-deep hole above the GPR hit. If there were remains down there, surely they'd find them soon.

Then one of the rangers paused in his digging. "I've got something."

She struggled to breathe as she crouched down next to the hole. A creamy brown knob protruded from the soil—a bone.

Bode propped his shovel against the side and mopped sweat from his forehead. He gestured to one of the rangers. "Karsten, hand me the trowel and the brush, will you? And bring the bags."

She watched as they meticulously brushed away the dirt and exposed what looked like a femur, judging by the length and diameter. One of the rangers grabbed a camera and took photographs to document the position of the bone. Then they tagged it and placed it in a bag.

More of the skeleton emerged as both Bode and the

other ranger kept clearing away the soil. The pelvis, spinal column and ribs stretched up to a mostly intact skull. The arms had been crossed across the victim's chest, as if he or she had been laid out in a coffin. Metal carabiners were pinned to each hand. Sky shifted her weight from one foot to the other, a giant fist gripping her rib cage.

Was this her father? If it was, shouldn't she feel it, somehow? Or had his spirit been gone so long that any sense of his presence had vanished?

"Agent Tucker, look at this," the ranger said from the other end of the hole. He tapped his trowel against something with a clang. Metal.

She sank down to her hands and knees, staring over the edge, as the photographer snapped pictures opposite her. Then Bode moved in front of her, blocking her view temporarily as he hunched over whatever they'd found. Every muscle locked into place like she'd been cryo-frozen. Her lungs wouldn't expand.

Then he moved back, turned and met her gaze. The look on his face said everything—hesitation, concern, sorrow.

"It's a prosthetic leg."

FIVE

Morning dawned too quickly, the sunlight blinding Skylar and making her puffy eyes sting. She exhaled a shaky breath then offered a silent prayer of gratitude that she'd lived to see another day. After startling awake in the night with dreams of being smothered, she'd glanced at the twin bed opposite her where Deputy Rachel Moore slept, her weapon and radio beside her on the nightstand, and felt a little better.

They hadn't finished excavating the remains yesterday until late, as they'd discovered a second set buried beneath the first, along with another carabiner. Sky had watched, arms wrapped across her stomach, as they carefully removed each bone. Her insides had felt numb by the time they were finished. Bode had had to rush away to pick up Harper, leaving one of the rangers to take the evidence to the ISB's crime lab. A deputy had escorted Sky to the chief ranger's office, where she met Rachel and moved into one of the park's semiprivate apartments with its own bathroom.

She was grateful for the solid walls and the extra protection but could've used the fresh air right now that had come with the tent cabin. The comforting feeling of being in nature. Maybe, in some tiny way, it made her feel a little bit closer to her dad.

Her chest squeezed, and she forced her feet out of bed. The thought that they might have finally found him, that after all this time she and her family might have answers… She still didn't know how to process it. Maybe she wouldn't, at least not until they'd identified the remains for sure. As she quietly gathered her things to get ready for the day, Rachel stirred.

"Hey, good morning. How did you sleep?"

Sky smiled, pushing aside the bad dreams and thoughts of her father that had kept her awake. "Better with you as a roommate. Thank you again for being willing to stay out here."

The other woman, who appeared to be in her mid-twenties, pulled her shoulder-length blond hair back into a ponytail. "Happy to help. I love it out here, and since I'm single, it's no biggie." She let out a soft, wistful sigh, then straightened her back. "What's the plan for today?"

"I'm meeting Agent Tucker at eight thirty a.m. at the ISB office. We're going over evidence and discussing next steps."

"Sounds good." The deputy stretched, letting a yawn slip out. "I'll escort you over and then check in with Sheriff Hart. Where do we get breakfast around here?"

"There's a dining hall in Curry Village. My groceries got left behind in the communal kitchen for the tent cabins, but they gave me an employees' meal plan card to get us through the week. Once things are back to normal, I'll be able to head out of the park to a grocery store." *If* things were ever normal again. Still, she felt a little better knowing someone cared. Bode and the chief ranger had made sure she was safe and had what she needed.

They arrived punctually at the ISB office, bellies comfortably full of eggs, bacon and hot coffee. Between the caffeine and the crisp mountain air, Sky felt more awake than she had since arriving in Yosemite.

"Good morning." Bode rose from his desk and waved them over.

Sky couldn't help glancing at the empty conference room where she'd had that impromptu dinner with Harper. She hadn't realized how much she'd missed being around children. Chris had gone out of his way to avoid them, so she'd stopped volunteering in the church nursery once they began dating more seriously. It had been enough of a challenge getting him *into* a church, much less getting him to stay there alone while she wrangled toddlers during the service.

"Thank you, Deputy Moore." Bode shook Rachel's hand. "I'll let you know when Skylar and I are wrapping up for the day."

Rachel nodded. "I'll check in with the sheriff and then probably head back to the crime scene." She left the way they'd entered.

Bode turned to Sky. "Sheriff's office called earlier. We've got an ID on the victim you saw the killer burying."

"Who was it?"

"A twenty-eight-year-old named Sharlene Foxx. She was reported missing four days ago by her friends. They were staying at Yosemite Lodge in El Portal."

How awful. What she'd intended as a nice getaway had turned into a nightmare. Sky pressed her hand to her sternum.

"This is why I do my job," Bode said grimly. "Once we catch this killer, he won't be able to hurt anyone else. Come on—" he gestured toward the hall "—let's go to the crime lab first." His expression softened. "Unless you'd rather not…"

She firmed her chin. "No, I need to. The sooner we find out, the better." Then she'd have to call Mom. The thought made her stomach churn. Maybe it'd be better to have her younger sister do it. Addie lived out in Missouri with her new husband. She'd only been five when their father vanished, too young to understand how it had broken up their family and wrecked their mother, the way Skylar knew. Addie had always gotten along with Mom better than Sky had. Maybe because Sky was the one who had had to pick up the slack and keep things together for all of them.

"This way." Bode placed a hand lightly against her back—no more than his fingertips—but the touch burned through her shirt even though he pulled away almost as soon as he made contact.

She blew out a quick breath, hoping the warmth in her cheeks wasn't making them turn red, the downside to having fairer skin. It wasn't like she'd never been around a man before—she *had* been nearly engaged, after all. It was silly, this effect Bode had on her.

The door to the crime lab opened as they approached, and a red-haired man who looked like he could bench-press Sky stepped out. "Hey, Bode." He held the door open.

"Graham, nice to see you back. What happened in Joshua Tree? Oh, and this is Skylar Jansen, Andy's daughter. Skylar, Special Agent Graham Burke."

She shook his hand, not at all surprised to find his grip strong and assured.

"Ranger Jansen, good to meet you." He glanced back into the lab, and his expression sobered. "And I'm so sorry for your loss. If anyone can find answers, it's this guy." He nodded toward Bode. "As for Joshua Tree, we caught the arsonist. He staged a wildfire to clear land for a development."

"That's awful." Sky frowned. She would never understand why people were willing to carelessly destroy nature for their own selfish ends. "I'm glad you caught the culprit."

"Me, too. Now to build the case for the prosecution." He waved a file folder at them and handed the door off to Bode before heading away down the hall.

The two sets of remains they'd recovered yesterday were spread out on an exam table, still contained in individual evidence bags. Sky's feet carried her straight to the prosthetic leg. She hadn't had time to examine it yesterday, but now she let her finger hover above the plastic bag. The surface of the metal was scratched and dirty, and there was no flesh-toned plastic cover—but then, her father had only worn the cover for special occasions.

"I'd like to send the skull to the forensic dentist at the local FBI crime lab," Bode said gently. "They'll be able to compare the teeth to available dental records."

"My father's, you mean?" She hated the way her voice hitched.

"Yes. I'm sorry, Sky. We'll run a DNA test on the other set."

Her eyes stung, and she blinked a few times. "It's better to know what happened. My mom never believed the story that he ran off with another woman, but I've watched the doubts eat away at her for years. She's never been able to put him to rest or move on."

He lifted a hand, almost as if he wanted to comfort her, then dropped it to his side. "That had to be so hard for you. Do you have siblings, too?"

"A younger sister, Addie. She's married now, working as a teacher out in Missouri. She was only five when he disappeared." Sky picked at the hem of her shirt. While her mom had been alternating between frantic searching and paralyzing grief, Sky had stepped in to take care of her sister and keep the family going. Little things like fixing her hair and making sure she had lunch for school. There hadn't been time to process her own feelings.

"You couldn't have been much older."

"Twelve. Old enough to feel his absence and all the ways the bottom dropped out of our family."

"Sky..." A muscle twitched in Bode's cheek. "I'm so sorry. No one should have to lose a parent." This time he did reach for her, squeezing her shoulder gently. He knew, didn't he? Maybe not how it felt to lose a parent, but his grief might even have been more painful. How had he managed not to fall apart the way her mom had?

She swiped at her cheeks. "Sometimes I hate living in a fallen world. How did you keep going, when your wife passed?" The question popped out before she'd really considered what she was asking from him. He might not want to be that vulnerable with her. "I'm sorry, I shouldn't have—"

"No, it's okay. Isla was diagnosed with a rare neuroendocrine cancer while she was pregnant with Harper. We started aggressive treatments right after the baby was born, but the outlook was never good. I knew it was coming, but that didn't make it easier. And after she was gone... I threw myself into my work. Reese saw how much I was struggling, and she kept me going. She and Jace and Graham." He scrubbed a hand over his face. "But I feel like I'm failing Harper. She lost her mom, and she hardly has me."

His words tugged at her heart. He was a good man, one who loved his daughter deeply. "Bode, I saw how you were with her. It's clear how much you love her. She knows that."

"Does Addie remember him?" His voice had dropped to a gruff whisper, and she knew he must be thinking about Harper.

A small smile tilted her lips. "She does. All the good

memories of hugs and tickles and stories read aloud. The warmth of being loved. Harper might not remember her mother, but she'll know she was loved."

"Thanks. The Lord has been faithful to take care of us." His Adam's apple bobbed, and he cleared his throat. "I guess we should get back to work?"

She nodded, swallowing the lump in her throat. The urge to wrap her arms around him and soothe away his pain nearly overpowered her, but she kept her hands firmly tucked at her sides. Despite how they'd just opened up to each other, they were colleagues. Two professionals working on a case together, nothing more.

Over the next hour, she helped him package up evidence to ship out, including the carabiners to be dusted for prints.

"What's next? Do we start interviewing suspects?" she asked when they'd returned to Bode's desk.

"I came up with a list the other night." He logged into his computer and clicked open a file. "A trail maintenance worker, a couple of seasonal employees… I need to pull up their employee records to see who we can rule out. Then we can do some informal interviews." His brows pulled together. "Are you sure about this? You've already experienced more than enough trauma."

She straightened her spine. "Yes, I'm sure. If my dad's killer is still on the loose, I'm going to do everything in my power to stop him."

Before anyone else got hurt.

Frustration churned through Bode's insides as he and Sky returned to his office later that afternoon. He had known his suspect list amounted to a wild-goose chase, but that didn't make it any easier to keep crossing off names. What he needed was a list of people who might've been in contact with Andy Jansen, but after everything Sky had gone through, he didn't want to overwhelm her with questions. They could wait a little longer until the analysis of the remains came back. Not to mention, it had been decades since her father worked in the park. How much would she remember?

Sky collapsed into a chair, brushing loose strands of hair out of her face. "What now?" She glanced at the clock. "What time do you have to pick up Harper?"

"Five. We've got a couple of hours." A sigh dragged out of his chest. "We need more to go on than just a name. Especially when it's most likely he would've lied about it."

She sucked her lower lip, and he forced his gaze away from her mouth. When she'd asked about Isla earlier that morning, for some reason he'd felt compelled to tell her. Maybe because he knew she'd understand his grief. But then, when he'd gone on about Harper and his own failures as a father… He gritted his teeth. Sky had been more than gracious about it, but he couldn't help feeling like he was pushing their working relationship into the wrong territory. The last thing he should be doing was opening up to her when he needed to guard his heart. And she was only in a seasonal position—maybe she'd be moving back to New York in a few months.

"What about my father?" Her question snapped him out of his dismal thoughts. "I know we haven't conclusively ID'd the remains, but what if we look for a connection with him? Obviously the killer knew him and knows I'm his daughter. Otherwise he wouldn't have left that note with me."

He rolled his chair closer to the desk. If she felt up to moving in that direction, he was ready. "Let me pull up your father's file. I have all the records from the original investigation."

A picture of Andy popped onto the screen as the file loaded. Bode glanced between the image and Sky, not missing the way her expression softened. "You two look alike."

Her eyebrows lifted. "You think? Everyone always said I look more like Mom. Probably because of the hair."

"You have the same eyes. And your smiles." He pointed at Andy, who was dressed in an NPS uniform and grinning for the camera. Farther down in the file, records listed everyone whom the investigators had interviewed. "Looks like the sheriff's office handled the case in conjunction with an ISB agent sent out from Washington, DC. That must've been before our branch was created."

The list was extensive—friends, family, coworkers. Anyone who might've seen or spoken with Andy in the days leading up to his disappearance. As he scrolled through it, Sky traced her fingers across one of her palms.

"That's a long list. What do we do, look up each person to see if they're still living in the area?"

He leaned back in his chair, letting out a short huff of breath. "Yep." It would take a long time, and time was one thing they didn't have. Not with a killer actively hunting her.

She sat up, snapping her fingers. "What about his climbing buddies? What if we start with them? I know the police would've pursued every angle, but maybe someone knows more than they were willing to share. It's been long enough now that they might talk. Especially to me. And we did find carabiners with the bodies."

"It's worth a shot." He glanced at his wristwatch. "We've got enough time for maybe one stop here in the Valley before I'll have to pick up Harper."

"Perfect. Let's head for Camp 4."

He raised an eyebrow. "How old were you when you moved away?"

"Fifteen." She chuckled, and the sound warmed his insides. "What? You're surprised I still remember where the climbers hang out? Dad pointed it out literally every time we drove past. He loved that place."

Bode led the way back out to his NPS vehicle and, after they'd climbed in, headed for the campground located near the Valley's most popular climbing areas. Even midweek in May, the place was packed with tents—some representing families, but most belonging to the climbing "dirtbags" who took up residency in Yosemite for the summer. He'd been one of them for a few seasons before he married Isla and took a job as an instructor.

This late in the afternoon, most of the occupants were back at the campground, tending to their gear or gathered around one of the campground's large boulders, watching each other scrabble their way up. A couple of kids played tag, darting over the tent stakes and somehow managing not to trip on the lines.

He parked his vehicle in the only open spot, one designated for rangers. After they climbed out, he pointed to a tent cabin just beyond the registration station. "Let's start with the camp host."

The door opened as they approached, and an older, gray-haired man in a volunteer shirt stepped out. He caught sight of Bode's uniform and waved. "Howdy, Ranger. What can I do for you?"

Bode introduced himself and Skylar, then shook the man's hand. He gave his name—Martin Drake—and told them he'd been volunteering in the park for the past several years since retiring as a full-time middle school teacher.

"That's wonderful, Mr. Drake," Sky said. "We're wondering if you might be able to help us."

"Please, call me Martin. How can I help?"

She glanced at Bode, as if waiting for him to decide how much they should reveal.

"We're working on a case that might be connected with the disappearance of a ranger nearly two decades ago. Andy Jansen? Maybe you've heard of him." When a puzzled expression passed over Martin's face, Bode kept going. "He loved climbing and was friends with several of the local climbers. The police interviewed them all back then, but we're wondering who might still be around. Can you point us in the direction of anyone who might know?"

"Well..." Martin dragged a gnarled hand across his chin. "There's been a few coming and going through the camp so far this season." He pulled his hand away and pointed toward a blue tent visible between the trees. "You know what? Why don't you try Walter Heinz? He's been around for decades. Even if he didn't know Andy personally, he could probably tell you who did."

After thanking Martin, they found Walter sitting outside his tent coiling a length of climbing rope. He wasn't as old as the camp host, but he appeared to be at least in his late fifties. Bode introduced them, and Walter invited them to join him.

"Sure, I knew Andy," he said as they took seats at a picnic table. His gaze lingered on Skylar. "Are you...related?"

Her cheeks flushed, but her lips tilted up. "I'm his daughter. I didn't think it was that obvious."

"I remember him bringing you around." He pointed to a huge nearby boulder. "You used to make it halfway up that before he'd notice and make you come back down. Do you still climb?"

She shrugged. “A little. Mostly indoors, but I’m hoping to get out while I’m here.”

An image popped into Bode’s mind of taking Sky to one of his favorite easier pitches. The two of them spending a morning together just having fun, challenging each other. It sounded glorious—but also far too much like a date. He clamped a lid on the thought and focused on Walter. “We’re working on a new case that might be linked to Andy’s disappearance. Did he have conflicts with any of the climbers? Any altercations you can remember?”

Walter surveyed the two of them. “The police came around asking all these questions back when he vanished.”

Bode settled an elbow on the table. “I have the files. But we were hoping someone who was reluctant to share back then might be willing to tell us more now.”

“Please.” Sky’s gentle tone tugged at his heart.

“Well, I suppose it don’t help to stay tight-lipped any longer, now that Jeremy’s gone, too.” At their surprised expressions, Walter went on. “Jeremy Flint. He was a handful, that one. Don’t know why the climbing community rallied around him as much as they did, other than he was one of their own, and your father was law enforcement. He and Andy had several run-ins over everything from incorrect permits to violating quiet hour regulations. Seemed like Jeremy had a new girlfriend every other week. One of them claimed he’d hit her, so she broke up with him. Never saw her again after that.”

Bode exchanged a glance with Sky. He didn’t recall anything about a Jeremy Flint in the police reports—certainly nothing to this extent, but then he hadn’t had time to read closely.

“What happened to Jeremy?” Sky leaned forward. “Where can we find him?”

"You can't, not anymore. He died in a climbing accident up at Tuolumne Meadows 'bout eighteen years ago. Would've been six months maybe after your father vanished." Walter shrugged. "Not an uncommon way for climbers to go, especially the overconfident ones."

Well, that didn't help. Unless he'd survived somehow? And turned into a serial killer? The whole thing felt too far-fetched. Still, it wouldn't hurt to dig deeper into what had happened between him and Andy. Maybe the killer after Skylar was linked to Jeremy somehow.

"Does Jeremy have any surviving family we could speak to? Or anyone here who knew him well?"

Walter gestured toward the parking lot. "He's got a brother, Steven, who still works for one of the climbing companies." He scratched the top of his head. "El Capitan Mountaineering, I think it is. Like me, he's too old to be a guide anymore, but he drives one of their vans. Should be bringing a group back from Tuolumne anytime now."

"Thank you." Skylar glanced at the parking lot. "Maybe we'll be able to catch him."

Bode offered Walter a business card as he climbed to his feet. "Feel free to call if you think of anything else that might be helpful."

As they walked away from the campsite, he raised his eyebrows at Sky. "What do you think? Did he seem familiar at all?"

She shook her head. "I mean, maybe from when I was a kid. But I feel sure he's not the killer. Too tall, and his mannerisms weren't the same. Although—" she gnawed her lip "—there's always the chance I won't be able to tell. If he's good at acting."

Bode placed a hand on her arm and squeezed gently before releasing. "You're a smart and brave woman, Sky. I know you'll do your best." As they watched, a white van pulled into the nearby parking lot. The words El Capitan Mountaineering School were written in large blue letters on the side, with a logo showing the famous cliff. "Look who's here."

She exchanged a glance with him, then picked up her pace. They lingered a few yards away as a handful of climbers piled out of the vehicle: a father with his teenage son, a young couple and a group of college students. The driver, a wiry man wearing a company ball cap, waved goodbye and closed the passenger doors behind them.

Bode's pulse kicked up a notch. The man fit the height and description Sky had described for their suspect. Next to him, Sky stiffened, as if she'd noticed the same thing.

Could Jeremy Flint's brother be the killer?

Sky forced in a couple of slow breaths, trying to calm her racing heart. Just because the man bore resemblances to the one she'd stumbled across burying a body didn't mean he was the same person. Plenty of men around here could fit that description.

The driver waved goodbye again to the climbing students. As he headed for the driver's-side door, Bode hailed him. "Excuse me, can we interrupt you for a moment?"

"Sure, just let me move the van out of the way." He pulled the vehicle over to the side, then climbed out, taking off his ball cap and tucking it into a back pocket to reveal dark hair tinted with gray at the temples. Late afternoon light gave his features a friendly glow as he smiled good-naturedly at them. "What can I do for you, Rangers? Is there a problem?"

"No problem, sir," Bode said. "We were hoping to ask you a couple of questions. Are you Steven Flint?"

The man nodded. "That's me." His gaze flitted across them, lingering for a moment on Sky. Did he recognize her? And in what capacity? As Andy Jansen's daughter, or as his next victim?

She shifted her weight, leaning closer to Bode's solid presence.

He responded by doing the same, until their arms were almost touching. A flood of gratitude filled her, both for his care and his strength. "Mr. Flint, we'd like to ask you a couple of questions about your brother, Jeremy. Can you tell us how he passed away?"

A shadow crossed Steven's face. "Yeah, it was eighteen years ago. He and I were climbing a pitch on Lembert Dome over at Tuolumne Meadows, one we'd done lots of times. Jeremy was on lead, and since it was an easy route, he skipped placing some cams where we should've put them." He glanced between them. "Cams are removable anchors climbers attach their ropes to, in case you're not familiar with the term. Anway, an afternoon storm popped up, and the route got wet. He missed a hold and fell maybe forty feet, striking the wall. I was able to lower him to a ledge and then climb to him, but by then it was dusk. He insisted we rappel down instead of spending the night up there. But..." He looked down at the ground for a moment, then cleared his throat. "Sorry, it's still hard after all these years."

"Of course," Bode soothed. "Take your time."

Steven drew in a slow breath. "We misjudged the amount of rope we'd need, and he fell. By then it was dark. I clung to the cliff all night until someone saw me the next day."

How awful. Compassion for his suffering burst beneath her ribs. "I'm sorry, Mr. Flint."

"You can call me Steven." The skin around his eyes

crinkled as he offered a small smile. "It was the worst day of my life."

"I take it there's no chance Jeremy survived the fall?"

Steven shook his head at Bode's question. "The EMT said he'd died on impact. Broken neck. They took the body away before I got down, and I didn't want to remember him that way, so I never made a visual identification." His brows pulled together. "Why are you asking?"

"We're working on a case and trying to follow all possible leads," Bode said. She couldn't help admiring his skillful tact. "Can we contact you if we have further questions?"

"Of course." The worried look hadn't left Steven's face. He handed them a card for the mountaineering school. "You can reach me through the school's number."

Bode took the card and added it to his pocket. "Thank you. And one last question, which pitch were you on when the accident happened?"

He described the location using details that didn't mean anything to Sky. Yet again, she was thankful Bode was here and that he had the expertise to understand exactly what Steven was talking about. As he spoke, Steven took the hat from his pocket and curled the bill under his hands. She couldn't help noticing they had the same wiry strength as the rest of him—the sort of hands that could easily strangle someone. But didn't all climbers have strong hands? And nothing about his manner seemed to indicate he'd met her before. Or had attempted to kill her.

After Steven had returned to his van, Bode nodded toward his vehicle. "That's all we have time for today. What do you think?"

She pursed her lips. "He's the right height and build, for sure. And he'd be strong enough…" The words trailed off as she shuddered, and a look of concern flashed across

Bode's face, but she waved him off. "I'm okay. He seemed legitimately upset about his brother, and nothing else gave off 'killer' vibes. And his voice..." *Had* it sounded like the killer's, maybe just a bit? She shook her head. The last thing she wanted was to condemn a potentially innocent man, and her encounter with the killer had been too brief to say for sure. "I don't know. What's your take?"

He unlocked his vehicle and opened the door for her, then walked around to the driver's side. When they'd both climbed in, he said, "I agree with your assessment, but I'd like to know more about their accident. It doesn't seem likely, but if Jeremy *wanted* to disappear, he could've faked his own death with the help of the EMT."

"Why, though? Because he'd already killed my dad and was afraid of being caught?"

Bode nodded. "Exactly. Or that girlfriend who broke up with him that Walter mentioned. If he was abusive to her, maybe he was afraid she'd press charges. I'll need to dig deeper into him. We can also contact the mountaineering school to ask more about Steven—what kind of employee he is, what his work schedule is like. That sort of thing."

She tapped at the clock on the dashboard. "Yikes, you'd better drop me off so you can pick up Harper. Where do we start tomorrow?"

"I'd like to pay a visit to Tuolumne Meadows to the site of their accident." A gleam sparked in his eyes. "How do you feel about a little adventure?"

SIX

A tiny thrill of anticipation danced up Sky's spine as she stared at the granite peaks towering above the trees.

Bode glanced at her, grinning. Like her, he was dressed in regular clothes instead of a uniform, similar to the day she'd met him. His blue shirt brought out the color of his eyes, a fact she wished she could avoid noticing.

"Magnificent, isn't it?"

She nodded. "I can't believe I lived away from it for so many years. I'd take that over a skyscraper any day." The gleam in his eyes made her cheeks flush. They weren't on a date; she shouldn't be hoping for his approval or fostering this growing connection between them. Not after the way Chris had led her on then dumped her for someone else. A nagging voice reminded her that Bode was nothing like Chris, but that didn't mean she could trust him not to break her heart.

This whole line of thinking was ridiculous anyway—he wasn't interested in her like that, not after he'd lost his wife.

She broke eye contact, adjusting the straps of her pack. "So, what's the plan?"

He pointed to a large granite dome that stood out like a bald head above the pine trees. "That's Lembert Dome. The Flints' accident happened on the side facing us. We'll have a short walk to the base. We won't climb their route, but there's one next to it that has some fixed anchors and is less challenging. Sound good?"

"Sounds perfect." Her gaze locked with his again for a moment before she jerked her attention back to the trailhead. It was far too easy to stare into his clear blue eyes.

Birds twittered in the evergreen branches overhead as they started up a trail leading from the parking area to the dome. It was still early enough in the season that the place wasn't crowded yet. Only a couple of vehicles sat in the parking lot besides theirs, including a classic orange Volkswagen van that looked like it had fallen out of a documentary on 1970s Yosemite climbing.

It was refreshing being away from the Valley, which was packed with visitors no matter how cool the temperatures were. And up here, where the elevation was higher, it was chilly. She tugged the sleeves of her fleece down over her hands, glad she'd thought to wear it. "Did you grow up near Yosemite?" she asked as they walked.

"No, northern Cali, actually. Close to the Oregon border. I didn't discover this place until I was in college and my buddies wanted to go climbing for spring break. It was love at first sight, as they say. From then on, I came back every chance I got."

"How did you—" *meet your wife?* She cut off the insensitive question before she blurted it all the way out.

"What?"

She cleared her throat, stalling until she could come up with something better to ask. "How did you earn a living before you became an ISB agent?"

"I worked as an instructor for one of the climbing schools. It's how I met Isla, actually. She was a middle school teacher at a private school out in Monterey and came with her students on a school trip. We hit it off and struck up a long-distance relationship, then tied the knot about a year later."

Wow... "That was quick. Especially since you didn't live near each other." Nothing like her and Chris. They'd dated nearly four years before she even began to hope he might propose.

He shrugged. "I guess we just knew."

"You were blessed, to have a relationship like that," she offered. It wasn't much, but it was the truth. "I dated a man in New York for over four years. He worked on Wall Street, one of those stereotypical Manhattan businessmen. High-rise apartment, designer suits. He gave me a Rolex for my birthday one year."

Bode shot her a quizzical look. "Really? You don't seem like the type who would..." He grew silent, maybe out of fear of offending her.

She laughed, though the sound came out more bitter than she'd intended. "I'm not. See?" She held up her wrist, which bore only a cheap digital stopwatch she'd picked up at the mall to use for timing her runs. "I sold it after he dumped me."

He winced. "I'm sorry."

"Me, too. After all those years together, I thought he was finally going to propose. But instead he took me out for a nice breakup dinner." She'd splurged on a gorgeous black chiffon dress, Kate Spade shoes, and jewelry for the occasion—blowing through a few months' worth of her clothing budget in one shopping trip. At least she'd recouped part of the costs through an online resale store.

Bode's brows furrowed. "What was *wrong* with him? Who treats a woman that way, especially one like you?"

Her shoulders curled as she shrugged, trying not to care.

But she did. Maybe the wound was still too fresh. "He said I wasn't who he thought I was and that we both needed the freedom to find the right match. Ultimately, I wasn't enough for him. He started dating another woman the next day." For a second, an image burned in her mind's eye of Chris with an elegant, dark-haired woman in a red dress, sharing an intimate candlelit meal in the Italian restaurant less than a block from Sky's apartment. Almost as if he'd wanted to be seen. Then reality crashed back in, and she clamped her mouth shut as heat burned up her neck. Why had she blabbed the whole sob story to Bode?

His hand touched her shoulder, and she stopped. "Skylar, I hope you don't believe it was your fault. I don't know this guy—*jerk* was more the word I had in mind—but I know you. And it's not your responsibility to 'be enough' for someone else. A strong, godly relationship is built on mutual respect and sacrificial love. It's about serving the other person, not looking out for yourself. Don't settle for less than that, okay?"

"Yeah. Thanks," she mumbled, willing away the fire burning in her cheeks. Now poor Bode felt obliged to dispense relationship advice to her. Note to self: *no more oversharing.*

The sound of voices ahead provided a welcome relief from her embarrassment. A few minutes later, the trail exited the cover of the woods as they reached the base of the dome, which sloped gradually upward over a rocky field toward a vertical granite face. Three climbers standing nearby glanced their way and waved. Far up the face, climbers moved like tiny ants ascending a wall. Her throat tightened.

"What do you think?"

She swallowed. "Where did you want to climb?"

"Not that high." He pointed to the specks far up the face and chuckled. "Those guys are on a long, multi-pitch route to the summit. We're doing a beginner's route. It starts at the same point as the route where Jeremy Flint fell, but veers in a different direction."

She scrambled after him up the sloping granite base for a short distance until the rock leveled out on a narrow shelf below the vertical wall. Long cracks ran upward, making her fingers itch to try them. She'd done a fair amount of crack climbing in the gym, but never on real rock. Adrenaline filtered through her system, and she had the distinct feeling that her nerves balanced on an edge and could go either way—excitement and fun, or spiraling toward a panic attack. *Deep breaths, Skylar.*

Bode set down their gear bag and scanned the wall in front of them. His gaze was sharp and attentive as he searched the rock for the section he wanted. It all looked the same to her. But his skill and knowledge made her feel safe, in a way she'd rarely felt with Chris. Not that he wasn't smart—he'd been brilliant at his job—but she'd spent most of the time with him feeling insecure. Like she couldn't measure up.

Even though he barely knew her, Bode never made her feel that way.

She shook off the thoughts she shouldn't be entertaining and glanced behind them at the way they'd come. A slip here wouldn't kill a person, but it would be a long, painful slide to the bottom. More climbers were on their way up, maybe to tackle routes in this same area.

"Where did—" She broke off when she realized Bode had picked his way a dozen feet farther to the left, examining the rock face above. She followed him.

"This is the route they were on." He pointed upward.

"See that deep vertical crack? Their route follows it to the top. Only three pitches, according to what Steven told me. They'd done harder routes farther down the face—" he gestured to the left "—earlier in the day."

To her it looked challenging, but to accomplished climbers like the Flints this route would've been easy. "How did they get into trouble, when they were such good climbers?"

"A little overconfidence can set you up for all kinds of poor choices, like not turning around when you should. Not setting cams. Not wearing a helmet. Then all it takes is one thing going wrong, and all your bad decisions pile up."

He'd been on a search-and-rescue team for the park service, hadn't he? How many such needless accidents had he seen?

"Could anyone survive the fall from up there?" The thought of smashing down onto this hard granite made her limbs ache. She inhaled a slow breath.

"Honestly, it depends on how he landed. The first pitch is a slab, which would either help or hurt depending on how you hit. And then the long scramble to the bottom..." He sucked his lower lip. "It looks survivable, but it depends on a lot of variables. We'll get a better view once we're up on the wall."

"What about the EMT who said he'd broken his neck?"

"There *is* that. And the fact they buried a body. People can get misidentified or mixed up in the morgue, but it's hard to imagine Jeremy Flint walking off and an EMT lying to cover for him."

She tugged on the end of her braid. "And if he'd survived, why *would* he walk off and not stick around to let his brother know he was alive? Or get help?"

Bode shook his head. "It doesn't make sense. Unless he wasn't getting along with his brother either and just wanted out? We know he'd had conflicts with your father and other climbers in the area. Maybe this was his opportunity to start over, so he faked an accident to convince Steven he died. Jeremy could've dropped right down onto his feet without a scratch."

"Maybe we can track down the EMT?"

"And I'll talk to Steven again to ask about his relationship with his brother and his alibi for the other day."

Her chest tightened. "Do you think…?"

"He's got the right build, for sure, but we don't have any other reason to suspect him at this point. It's not much to go on." He scrubbed a hand through his hair. "Let's get on the wall to get a better look before we head back. You still up for it?"

"Absolutely." Especially if this climb might help them catch a killer.

Bode moved slowly and carefully as he worked his way up the face, frequently glancing back at Sky to make sure she looked comfortable. The route was one of the easiest in Tuolumne Meadows, with plenty of ledges and sections that were more scrambling than climbing. But if she enjoyed it, he could always take her out on something more difficult.

Hold up, Tucker. Why was he even thinking along these lines? They were out here for the case. In fact, the whole reason they were together at all was because her life was in danger—not because they were dating or friends or… something.

Colleagues was the word he needed to remember. That and *professional*. Just because it was easy to be himself and open up with her didn't mean he needed to keep doing it.

Rock crumbled beneath his fingers, setting loose a surge of adrenaline as he tightened his hold with his other hand.

He needed to get his head in the game and focus on what he was doing. As the Flints had proven, even easy climbs could be dangerous out here.

"You okay?" Sky called up to him. She stood on a ledge about forty feet below as he worked his way through the third pitch, ready to belay, or lower, him if he slipped. A long line of blue rope stretched between their harnesses, hooked by carabiners to some cams he'd placed in the wall.

"Yep, all good. You're gonna love the view from up here." He'd climbed high enough to gain a panoramic view of the meadow, with granite domes and peaks rising on the opposite side. Far to the west, clouds pooled like fluffy cotton balls tossed into a bag. There'd be rain later, but they had plenty of time to get in a morning climb.

He took another cam from his sling then pulled back the spring-loaded lever, fitted it in and released it. Two metal pieces popped apart, wedged firmly in the rock. When Sky climbed up after him, she'd pull them out on her way. He clipped into the loop at the end and kept going, working his way to the left. Now that he'd gotten this high, it was time to take a closer look at where Jeremy Flint had allegedly fallen to his death.

He glanced back at Sky. "I'm veering off course just a little to check the route over there."

"Okay," she called back.

He worked his way carefully, testing each foothold with a little pressure before applying his full weight. This section had decent grips, which helped. As he rounded a protrusion in the rock, the granite face came into view, stretching hundreds of feet to his left, dotted intermittently with climbers.

He studied the rock wall, glancing down along the steep face to the flatter scramble far below. Rappelling off the end of the rope would've left Jeremy a long, hard fall. But to be honest, it seemed like too much of a rookie mistake, especially on a route this simple. Yes, overconfidence could've been a factor, but something felt off. Could Steven have been involved in staging—or causing—the accident in some way? His grief had seemed legitimate, but Bode would be wise to find the original reports. See if the authorities had felt a need to investigate. Or had Jeremy faked the fall and landed like a cat?

Bode's mind churned over the possibilities as he worked his way back around the protrusion. Sky waved to him from below, where she waited on the ledge with one hand firmly gripping the line strung between them. But as he stretched for the next grip, the rock broke loose beneath his fingers.

It took a split second to realize he'd lost his balance and that the toehold he had wouldn't be enough. "Falling!" he called as he lost contact with the rock face.

"I've got you!"

The line went taut, and he braced for impact as his shoulder hit the wall six feet below the last cam he'd placed. Ouch, that would leave a bruise.

"You all right?" Sky asked.

"Yeah—"

Suddenly there was a scaping of metal, and with a soft pop, the cam sprang loose from the crack. His body plunged before he even had time to call out.

A sharp scream pierced the air.

He dropped below the next cam, bracing to hit again, except as soon as the line tightened, it tore out of the wall, too. Adrenaline burned through his veins like lightning, and his feet scrabbled against the rock, trying to stop the mad descent as more of his cams broke loose like a giant zipper being unzipped. Finally he collided with a ledge, his knees buckling under the impact. Off balance, he nearly fell backward but managed to grip the rock and pull himself against it.

"Bode?" Sky's voice was laced with panic, and it was a whole lot closer than it should've been.

He shook off the cobwebs crowding his senses, grateful that he'd chosen early on to always wear a helmet, no matter how easy the climb. His stomach hollowed out when he realized she'd been yanked off her feet by his sudden free fall, even though they'd anchored her with cams from below. Now she dangled a few feet away to his left, her anchor lines hanging loose. Overhead, their line still looped through one cam that hadn't unzipped when the others did. *Thank You for that one, Lord.* Otherwise, they might've plunged the entire way down the cliff face.

"You okay?" he asked.

Her knuckles were white around the rope at her waist, and she stared down below, where her feet hung over open space.

"Skylar, look at me." The words came out harsher than he'd intended, but they got her attention.

Her eyes snapped to his, wide and unfocused. Her face appeared pale and clammy, and her chest moved up and down too rapidly.

"Hey, calm down," he said, more gently this time. "We're okay. We're going to be fine." He nodded, and she mirrored his movement, then took a deep breath.

"What do we do now?" Her voice was tight, but the focus had returned to her eyes. "My anchors pulled out."

"I see that," he said grimly. What was wrong with his cams? He took excellent care of his equipment, and the placements had been solid. They shouldn't have unzipped the way they had. Had someone tampered with them?

He shelved the disturbing thought. What mattered at

this exact moment was getting her to safety. Right now the only thing preventing her free fall was a lone cam and his weight on this two-foot-deep ledge.

"I'm going to reach for you and pull you over to me. Okay?"

She nodded again, lips pressed into a tight line.

He dropped onto his stomach on the ledge, keeping his center of gravity low and toward the wall. He held out his hand to her, and she stretched toward him, a few inches of space still separating them.

"Can you pull yourself closer?"

"I..." She stared down at the ground again, pressing her hands to her chest as she clutched the rope. "I..."

"Skylar, I need you to look at me. Now."

Her chest was moving too fast again, and a sheen of sweat glistened on her forehead. She'd be in danger of suspension trauma and passing out from poor blood circulation if she stayed in that position much longer, with her legs unsupported.

"Please, Sky. You can do this. I've seen your strength."

Finally she looked at him, the whites of her eyes huge around her green irises.

"Pull yourself toward me. Use the crack right there." If the mere force of his will could get her to move, he would do everything in his power to save her. *Help her, Lord.* Otherwise, he'd have to try climbing up the face to create enough slack to lower her down to the ledge beneath her, trusting all their weight to one cam.

He gritted his teeth, waiting, fingers reaching for her.

Then finally her throat bobbed, and she forced her attention to the rock face. Her fingers reached for the crack and dug in, straining as she pulled herself toward him. Finally his hand wrapped around hers, cool and slick with sweat, but he tightened his grip and pulled her toward him until her feet found the ledge.

As he moved into a sitting position to give her more room, she collapsed onto the rock next to him. She started leaning over as if she were going to lie down, but he kept her upright, locking an arm firmly around her shoulders.

"Nope. The blood has been pooling in your legs. We need to give it time to work back up to the rest of you without flooding your system."

She nodded, taking several slow breaths, before suddenly turning and stuffing her face into his shoulder. He held her close for a long moment, breathing in the sweet scent of her shampoo wafting through the holes in her helmet.

When she pulled away, she placed a hand to her chest. His arms felt suddenly empty. "Thanks. And sorry about that. I don't know what happened. I felt lightheaded all the sudden, like I was going to be sick. I'm not usually afraid of heights."

"It was probably the harness. You're used to wearing one when you climb in a gym, but you're only hanging from it for seconds on your way down. Suspension trauma can set in within minutes, especially for someone small." She *was* small, and the urge to pull her close and protect her hit him like a ton of bricks. But that would be completely counterproductive to his goal of keeping their relationship professional. How had the lines gotten so blurred, anyway? Why had his heart let down its guard so willingly?

She stretched her legs and arms one at a time, mindful of their precarious perch. "What happened? Why did the cams pull out?"

"I don't know. They were placed correctly." He held one up to show her, where they were still attached with carabiners to the rope at his waist. Equipment malfunctions were rare, especially given the care he took of his gear. He'd had to borrow climbing shoes and a harness for Sky, but he'd used his own cams. "Wait a sec..."

He unclipped the first one, turning it around in his hands. The metal cam lobes that spread apart to fit into the rock looked fine, but the closer he looked at the springs, the more he frowned. Inside the device's shaft, three of the four springs were broken. And from the perfect nature of the breaks, "cut" might be a better word for it.

"Look at this. The springs are damaged. The one intact spring provided enough tension for me to place the cam, but the broken ones couldn't support my weight."

Sky's brows pulled together. "What about the other ones?"

One at time, Bode inspected each shaft. Exactly the same—one intact spring, three cut. There was no way this was an accident.

The way the blood drained from her face showed she'd reached the same conclusion. "Somebody sabotaged our gear," she whispered.

Which meant...the killer knew they were out here. And he was tracking their every move.

SEVEN

Bode stole a quick glance at Sky as he took another bite of his chicken sandwich. She'd been a real trouper that morning, between her willingness to tackle the climb in the first place and then her bravery on the descent. They'd been totally exposed on that cliff, but they'd managed to get down in one piece.

Now, after changing into uniform, they sat in his office stuffing down a late lunch before figuring out next steps. Outside, clouds were building to the west as a storm front swept closer to the park.

"Who had a chance to tamper with your gear?" Her red hair hung in loose waves around her shoulders, pretty against the soft gray of her uniform. *Not* that he should be noticing. "We left the bag unattended for a few minutes. Do you think one of the other climbers could've done it?"

He swallowed a bite of food and washed it down with a swig of water. "If someone had the right tool and knew exactly what they were doing, it wouldn't take long to make the cuts." After they'd gotten back to the parking lot, he'd checked over all his cams—half of them had been cut. A sad waste of his gear, and it had nearly cost them their lives. "I was so focused on the wall I wasn't paying attention. Did you see anyone come close?"

He hated admitting that fact, but climbers—and most outdoors sports types—trusted each other with their lives, even strangers. It wasn't unusual to leave one's gear unattended.

"Yes, there were a couple of climbers who walked past our stuff. Both men, I think. One had a red helmet." She shook her head. "But I wouldn't feel confident trying to identify them."

"All right. I can ask around and try to find out who was at Lembert this morning." The other possibility, the one he really didn't want to think about, was that someone had sabotaged the cams earlier. He tended to keep his gear bag in either his personal vehicle or his NPS SUV to have it at the ready. Had the perp found an opportunity to access it last night? Or the day before? The idea of a killer lurking near his home, or breaking into his car, with Harper's car seat right there, made the hairs rise on the back of his neck.

"Steven Flint knew we would be out climbing. Who else knew?"

"I borrowed your shoes and harness from a friend who works for Yosemite Mountaineering School. Someone might've overheard our conversation. But I think we need to dig a little deeper into the Flints."

She straightened, her eyes going wide. "What about that morning we met? You left your gear behind when we ran for the road."

Yes, he had, hadn't he? The killer would've seen it sitting there, unattended. "You're right. It sat for a couple of hours before I got back." He balled up the wrapper from his lunch, squeezing it in his fist. "I'm sorry, Sky. I check over all my gear before I climb, but it never occurred to me examine the springs in my cams."

She shook her head. “It’s not your fault. Why would you anticipate sabotage?”

His phone rang as he tossed the balled wrapper into the trash can.

“Maybe we’ve got news.” He flashed the phone at Sky, showing the caller ID as the regional crime lab, then accepted the call and put it on speaker. “Special Agent Bode Tucker.”

“Agent Tucker, this is Bonnie Weisma from MCCA Laboratories. I’ve got your DNA results and forensic dental analysis for human remains you sent us on a rush order. I’ll be sending the full report to the email you provided.”

“That was fast, thank you. What’ve you got?” His gaze went to Sky, who shifted nervously in her seat. Almost without thinking, he reached for her hand and held it.

“Three victims. The first is female, twenty-seven years old. Carly Brumstead. Estimated death between fifteen and twenty years ago. Then a male, forty-two years old.” Papers rustled, as if she were double-checking the name, and he squeezed Sky’s hand gently. “Andrew Jansen.”

Sky’s fingers tightened around his, and her other hand went to her mouth.

“Estimated death also fifteen to twenty years ago,” she went on. “And the third is Payton Smith, female, twenty-five years old, estimated death between five and ten years ago.”

“Thank you, Ms. Weisma. I’ll look for the full report in my inbox.” He kept his gaze on Sky as he spoke, wishing there were some way to ease her pain.

“One more thing,” the woman added. “The carabiners you sent—the three found with Payton Smith, Sharlene Foxx, and Skylar Jansen—had no prints, but the carabiners found with Carly Brumstead and Andrew Jansen did. We were able to find a match in IAFIS." Sky's grip on his hand tightened. "It's for a deceased man named Jeremy Flint."

His pulse flared but he thanked the lab tech, released Sky's hand and ended the call. When he turned to her again, she had both hands pressed to her mouth, her gaze staring past him to a spot on the ceiling. He knew how she felt. In a span of seconds, they'd learned the answer to a cold case that had haunted his office for nearly two decades.

"You okay?" he asked gently.

She pulled her hands back, her gray-green eyes flitting to him, and nodded. "We know what happened. Well, not exactly... But my dad must've made Jeremy Flint angry enough that he killed him. He didn't run off with some woman. He was murdered. I need to call my mom."

"Of course. You can use the conference room to have some privacy." A piece of string looped around his heart, tugging uncomfortably as he watched her stand. She had to be going through a maelstrom of emotions, and the oddest feeling had come over him—as if he wished *he* could be the one to tuck her in close and comfort her, the way he'd consoled Isla when her older sister nearly died in a traumatic car accident. But that wasn't the kind of relationship he had with Sky, nor did he want it. *Right?* He swallowed his confusion and waved at the computer screen. "I'll do some research, and when you get back, we can plan our next steps."

The unsettled feeling lingered as he pulled up the county coroner's contact information. Solving complex cases was hard enough without dragging personal emotions into things. He needed to shake off this sense of longing, or whatever it was, and get his head back in the game. If Jeremy Flint had murdered Andy Jansen and Carly Brumstead, then who had killed the other victims? And who was after Sky? Either Jeremy had, in fact, survived—*or faked*—his accident, or they had a copycat killer on their hands who knew what Jeremy had done. Steven Flint? Or a close friend of Jeremy's?

And if Jeremy was still alive, whose body had been sent to the coroner? And who had assisted him with faking his death? The EMT? Or had it been Steven, who then lied to cover it up?

He tapped through to the coroner's office, and an assistant answered after a couple of rings. "This is Special Agent Bode Tucker calling from the ISB office in Yosemite. I'm wondering if you have fingerprints on file for a victim in a climbing accident from several years ago. Name Jeremy Flint, age thirty-seven at the time."

"Let me check." Clicking sounds came through the phone as the assistant typed out the information, then a pause. "No, I'm sorry, we don't have any prints for him. It says here the body came in identified, so they wouldn't have been taken. You could check with the funeral home, though. I'll forward you the information."

He thanked the assistant then hung up, glancing over at the conference room. Sky stood with her back to him, phone pressed to her ear. Where had she said her mother lived? Her sister lived in another state, he remembered that much. *Focus*, he reminded himself. Details about her family weren't relevant to the case.

He would need to put together a statement for the press, though. This case had hung over the park's proverbial head for nearly two decades, and when the news broke, it would go big. Chief Kleinman and Reese would want to know, too. Bode took a moment to make a quick call to each of them, promising a press release as soon as he could get it written.

An email popped into his inbox from the lab with the

contact information for the funeral home. He tapped in the number and connected with a receptionist, who promised to check their records. Maybe then he and Sky would be able to resolve the question of who had been buried, if it wasn't Jeremy Flint.

By the time Sky returned, he was knee-deep in the park's incident reports, trying to find any clue that might indicate who the EMTs were that responded to the Flints' accident.

"Hey." Her soft voice pulled him out of his concentration.

He swiveled in his chair as she took a seat, gripping his armrests to keep from reaching for her. "How did it go? If you need to go home, I can hold down the fort here. Might even be safer."

Or not, given how much the killer seemed to know about her.

She shook her head. "Addie is going to fly home to San Bernardino to stay with Mom for a few days. We all agreed it's best for me to help bring Dad's killer to justice."

"If he's still alive. Sky, there's the chance it's a copycat after you now. Someone who knows what Jeremy did."

"But the notes he left me… And he told me his name was Jeremy. Whoever it was knew my father and knows we're related. But why would someone else fake he was still alive? And then come after me?"

He scrubbed a hand over the stubble on his chin. "Those are good questions. And then we have the other victims. If I log into the NamUs—" he clicked through and typed in a name "—here's Carly Brumstead. Vanished six months before your father. Then Payton Smith, who disappeared six years ago. She worked at a hotel in Wawona. Sharlene was too recent to be listed. There are big gaps between the murders. So if it is Jeremy, what prompted him to resume the killings? And if it isn't, why is someone trying to frame him?"

"Are the victims connected in any way? Besides the carabiners found with the bodies?" Her gaze drifted to the ceiling as if she were lost in thought. It occurred to him how much he appreciated this conversation—all their conversations, really. How he could bounce ideas and questions off her and she never seemed to miss a beat.

"They're all local, and other than your father, female." He drummed his fingers on the desk. "There's also the possibility more victims exist who haven't been found yet. We know the killer likes using that clearing, but he could've left remains elsewhere also."

She lifted a finger. "Especially if he left the area for a while. If Jeremy Flint did fake his own death, maybe he moved afterward to start over with a clean slate. You know, changed his name, got a job, that sort of thing." Her brows pulled together. "How do you get employment with a fake name?"

"It's not as hard as you'd think, unfortunately. Anyone who could fake their own death could find ways to get fake identity documents, too."

"What about the EMTs who responded to the Flints' accident? Can we figure out who was there?"

"I was just working on that. Since the incident occurred in the park, the dispatch records should be in the Case Incident Reporting System. Yosemite has an internal EMS service that would've responded." As much as he loved the natural world, he had to admit modern technology was brilliant sometimes. Within a few minutes, he found the incident report and had two names on the screen: one for the ambulance driver and the other for the paramedic.

"Wait a sec..." Sky pointed toward the screen, her finger

hovering near the names. "That paramedic's name looks familiar. Kathryn Hillsburg. Can you get a photograph?"

"Should be able to." He opened a separate tab and pulled up an employee records database. After he typed in the name, a picture appeared onscreen of a blond woman with her hair tied back in a ponytail over a tall forehead.

Sky made an almost strangled sound, pressing her hand to her mouth.

"What's wrong?" The blood had drained from her face.

"That's the woman who a witness claimed my father got into a car with the last day he was seen. Authorities never found her to question her. Bode, she's tied to this case. I know it."

Sky wiped her sweat-slicked palms against her pants. Kathryn Hillsburg stared back at her from the computer screen. Had she known Jeremy had killed Sky's father? Maybe he'd killed her, too, and that was why she'd never resurfaced.

"Wait, are you sure you remember what she looked like? It's been a long time."

"Yes, I'm sure. After the witness came forward, people tried to convince my mom Dad was having an affair. With her." She pointed at the picture. "Whether she knew it or not, Kathryn Hillsburg caused my family a lot of extra grief." Sky's chest ached at the memory of hearing her mother crying in the next room late at night. Mom had never openly doubted Dad's faithfulness, but the contradictory opinions offered by family, friends and the media had stung, making their confusing loss even more painful.

"How do you know who it was? I mean, did the witness provide her name? Or a physical description? Actually—" he turned to the computer "—I can look it up in the report."

"Yes, I believe her name was given via an anonymous tip. Also, security camera footage showed her at a gas station outside the park the night Dad vanished. There was a passenger in the vehicle, but the footage was too grainy to make an identification." She waited as he scrolled through page after page of documentation.

"Yep, there it is. An anonymous call to our tip line from a witness who claimed he or she saw Andy Jansen get into a silver Toyota Camry. Let's look for the video footage." He clicked a link and pulled up a grainy, black-and-white video in a separate window.

They watched as a light-haired woman got out of a Toyota Camry to pump gas. Someone who appeared to have dark hair shifted in the passenger seat, barely visible through the vehicle's front window.

Sky squinted at the computer screen. "How could they even identify Kathryn? This footage is awful."

Bode shrugged. "The FBI has a filtering system that can clean it up a little. My guess is they made the ID based on the front license plate."

"That makes sense. Good thing they're required in this state." She tucked her hair behind her ears, staring at the video as it looped on repeat. "Who's in the passenger seat? Jeremy Flint? Maybe someone mistook Jeremy for my father."

"If Kathryn had a relationship with him, that would explain why she'd help him disappear. I called the funeral home, and they're checking to see if they took prints from Jeremy's body. Steven never visually identified him, and the funeral was closed casket, so we can at least verify who they buried. In the meantime—" he reached for his phone "—we need to talk to Steven Flint again. Find out just how involved he was in his brother's disappearance and what he knows about Jeremy and Kathryn."

Sky leaned back in her chair, staring at the ceiling panels overhead while Bode waited for Steven to answer. What had happened to her father that day? Had he gone for a climb, the way she'd gone for a run, and found Jeremy Flint burying a victim, like Carly Brumstead? Maybe her father had had the same horrifying experience, only he hadn't been able to get away.

"Mr. Flint?" Bode asked into the phone. "This is Agent Bode Tucker. We have a few more questions for you. Wondering if we can schedule another interview." He switched the call over to speaker so she could hear.

"Sure, I'd be happy to. I have half an hour now before I need to go pick up a group. I can't be late, with the storm coming, but I'm near park headquarters if you'd like me to swing by."

Bode exchanged a glance with her, maybe thinking the same thing: Steven Flint was being very cooperative. "Sounds good. I'll meet you out front." They hung up, and Bode clasped his hands.

"Does he know something's up? Or are we about to surprise him?" She picked at her fingernails.

"I'm going to escort him to the interview room, where we can record him. I'll have you wait outside, okay? Just in case." His jaw clenched. "I'm not positive we should trust Steven Flint. He might be more involved than he seems."

"All right."

Fifteen minutes later, she stood outside the two-way mirror that provided a window into the small interrogation room. Graham Burke, one of the ISB agents she'd met earlier, had stopped by to join her when Bode apprised him of the latest updates on the case. Inside the room, Steven sat in the chair opposite the door, one knee bouncing up and down like a jackhammer, while Bode poured two cups of coffee from a pot in the corner.

"So this is the brother?" Graham leaned against the wall, arms crossed over his chest. Even though she didn't think Steven posed a threat, there was something comforting about having Bode and Graham right here.

She nodded. "He's got a squeaky-clean record, according to Bode. Other than the climbing accident."

"I guess we'll see what he has to say." He grew quiet as Bode handed Steven a cup and took the opposite seat.

"I know this isn't the most comfortable space," he said to Steven, "but I appreciate being able to record your answers for our records."

"Sure." The other man glanced at his watch. "But I do need to leave in twenty minutes to stay on schedule. What can I do for you?"

"We received some information today that implicates your brother Jeremy in the death of Andy Jansen."

Steven set down his cup of coffee and pressed a hand to his forehead. "Jeremy had a bad temper. And a hard time controlling himself. I'm sure you've heard that from others in the climbing community. He was known to take things a step too far on occasion. Please give Mr. Jansen's family my condolences."

"Thank you. I will." Bode shifted in his chair but never glanced her way, no doubt to maintain the illusion that she wasn't standing outside the room observing everything. "What can you tell me about a woman named Kathryn Hillsburg?"

Steven blinked, then took a sip of his coffee. "The name sounds vaguely familiar. Was she associated with my brother?"

"That's what we're hoping you could tell us."

He ran a hand over his short, dark hair. "Jeremy had a lot of different girlfriends. Maybe it was the volatile temper, but he had a hard time sticking with one person for long. I'm sorry, I can't really remember other names. In case you haven't been able to tell, we drifted apart after the first few years living in the area." A shadow passed over his face, and his jaw took on a hard set. "Jeremy wouldn't see eye to eye with me about a lot of things. He moved out into his own place, took on part-time jobs as a handyman. We'd still climb together, but we didn't have a lot in common."

"Who else might Jeremy have confided in? Who was he close to, if it wasn't you?" Bode propped his elbows on the table.

"Maybe one of his many girlfriends?" Steven laughed bitterly. "We were twins, after all. I always wanted to be close to him."

Twins? If they were identical, that would explain why the man who'd attacked her reminded her so much of Steven. Somehow Bode kept his face passive as he waited for Steven to take a sip of coffee.

"He had a couple of buddies who liked to party with him when they weren't climbing or working," Steven went on. "Jeff Reynolds and Scott… Siefert? Simmons? Something like that. They'd drive out to some remote place with a couple of girls, their gear and a case of beer. Party until a ranger busted them."

Like her father. She balled her hands into fists.

Bode jotted notes on a piece of paper. "I know you said he had several, but can you remember any of the girlfriends' names?"

"Oh, I don't know." Steven leaned back, placing his hands behind his head and looking up at the ceiling. "The one that stuck around the longest was Clara? Carly? I think it was Carly."

Sky's pulse quickened, and Bode glanced up sharply at Steven.

"Brumstead?" he prodded.

Steven shrugged. "Sounds right, but it's been years. Rumor was that he hit her and she was going to press charges, but she must've let it go because she just sort of vanished." He straightened, mouth going slack. "You don't think he…?"

Bode clicked off his pen and stuck it into a shirt pocket. "Thank you, Mr. Flint. I want to be respectful of your time." Both men stood.

"One more thing," Bode added as he reached the door. "Where were you on the morning of the twenty-third around seven a.m.?"

"When was that, Monday? I had a group to pick up at nine a.m., so I would've been home getting ready at that time. Why?"

"No reason, Mr. Flint. We'll be in touch if there are any new developments."

Sky waited with Graham as Bode walked Steven back out to the front of the building.

"How you doing with everything?" Graham asked.

She wrapped her arms across her stomach. "It's been a lot, but it means so much to my family to finally have answers."

He offered a kind smile. "I'm glad you could get some." When Bode arrived, Graham clapped his hand in one of those universal greetings all men seemed to know. "Tucker, let me know if there's anything you need. I'll be in and out over the next couple of days."

"Thanks, Burke."

"You should see Henlow in her rodeo getup. Apparently she's going undercover in Canyonlands."

Bode laughed. "Reese? Does she even know how to ride?"

"Don't you two doubt it. I'm a natural." Reese Henlow appeared in the doorway dressed in jeans and a plaid button-down, making the petite blonde look far more down-to-earth than she had in her uniform. She dashed over to her desk and grabbed an envelope. "Almost forgot this. Now, if you'll excuse me, I have a plane to catch. And Skylar, stick with Agent Tucker. He'll keep you safe and find justice for your family."

Sky glanced from Reese to Bode to see color creeping up into his cheeks.

He cleared his throat. "Just doing my job, boss." The way he enunciated each word hinted at some prior conversation, and Sky couldn't help wondering what exactly they'd talked about. Regardless, there was no doubt she felt safer with Bode than she did with anyone else.

After Reese waved goodbye and Graham returned to his case, Sky and Bode sat in front of his computer once more. "I'll have to pick up Harper soon." He glanced at his watch. "But I want to look up Jeremy Flint's two friends before we leave."

"What did you think of Steven's alibi, and the two of them being twins?"

"Interesting about the twins. We'll keep that fact tucked away. And as for the alibi, we'll have no way to confirm it other than making sure he showed up for work on time. Unless a neighbor happened to see him leave his apartment. According to our records, he lives alone."

Bode logged in and in a matter of minutes pulled up records and photographs for both men Steven had named. Jeff Reynolds had received a number of citations before being arrested for multiple counts of DUI. After serving a five-year sentence, he'd moved to Tennessee.

"He doesn't look anything like the Flints." Sky shook her head. "Unless he dyed his hair and lost a lot of weight. So he probably isn't playing copycat killer. What about the other one?"

"There's not a Scott Seifert, but here's Scott Simmons." A picture appeared on the screen of a man in his late forties with a thin face, scraggly mustache and bald head. "He had his share of citations, too, but he appears to have left the climbing scene. Current address is in Fresno."

She squinted at the picture, trying to imagine him with a ball cap and a shovel. "Maybe…? But why?"

"I think it's worth interviewing him. At a minimum, he might be able to tell us more about his history with the Flints." When she nodded, he added, "I'll try to set something up for tomorrow or the next day. For now, it's probably time to—"

A birdcall chimed from his phone. He glanced down at it, frowning. "Sorry, let me get this. It's Harper's school. Hello?"

Sky grabbed her handbag and tucked her water bottle and phone back into it. After the long day they'd had, a hot shower and bed sounded marvelous. But then Bode's tight words cut through her thoughts of relaxation.

"What? I'll be there right away." He clicked off the call and stood, one hand gripping the edge of the desk.

"What is it? Is Harper all right?" Sky slipped the strap of her bag over her shoulder and rose to her feet.

His gaze met hers, and the fear churning in the depth of his blue eyes made her knees go weak.

"I don't know. She's missing."

EIGHT

"Missing? How?"

Sky's concerned words barely penetrated the buzzing in Bode's head. He grabbed his phone, his keys… His side-arm was in its holster. Anything else could wait. He was supposed to take Skylar back to her lodging, but maybe Rachel could meet her here.

"Can you call Deputy Moore to come get you? I need to go."

She shook her head, starting for the door. "I'm coming with you. What's going on?"

Maybe he shouldn't let her tag along, but that fact didn't stop the sweet sense of relief filling his chest. Right now, he didn't want to be alone.

"Okay." As he headed for the door, he shared what little he knew. "They took the kids outside for recess an hour ago. It's fenced, a nice little playground next to the building. The kids all know how to line up on the colored dots when it's time to come in." Harper always followed her teachers' directions. They'd told him so over and over: what a sweet, obedient child she was.

A vise gripped his ribs as he held the door for Sky. After exiting, he clicked the key fob to unlock the doors for his personal vehicle, and they climbed inside. "When they got back indoors, she wasn't there. Wasn't with the group." Pain seared his throat, threatening to choke him, until a cool hand rested on his arm.

"Bode, look at me." He struggled to turn his head, to force his attention onto Sky's face. The buzzing was growing louder, making it hard to think. She released his arm, then reached over, cupping her hands around his cheeks. Her fingers felt cool against his skin. "We are going to find Harper. You and me. Okay? You drive, and I'll pray."

"Okay," he breathed. The noise in his brain receded as he exhaled. She pulled back, buckling her seat belt, and he started the engine. As he drove, he registered the soft sound of her voice somewhere in the background of his thoughts. Praying, asking the Lord to look after Harper and to help them find her.

Her quiet murmuring grounded him as he wove through traffic toward the day care center. He pulled into a spot, cut the engine and beelined for the door with Sky on his heels.

The receptionist jumped to her feet as he rushed inside, a worried look creasing her forehead. It was nearing 4:30 p.m.; other parents would be arriving soon to collect their kids, but right now they had the reception area to themselves.

"Mr. Tucker." She reached for the phone. "I'll notify Ms. Breton you're here."

A moment later, the director of the center emerged from the hallway. "Mr. Tucker, I'm so sorry. Please come in to my office."

He and Sky followed the older woman, passing by Harper's classroom. Laughter drifted out from beneath the door, chafing his raw heart. He couldn't help glancing through the window as he passed, as if maybe they'd made a mistake and his little girl was still there. But she wasn't, and only the steadying presence of Sky kept him upright.

Harper needed him to stay strong.

"Let's start with the security footage." Ms. Breton swiveled her screen around so they could see. She offered him and Sky seats, but he couldn't sit. Not when Harper was missing.

"Here's the footage starting at three thirty p.m. when they went outside." On her screen, multiple black-and-white videos played simultaneously for the building's different security cameras. The children in Harper's classroom lined up inside, following their teacher out. They dispersed across the playground, but he kept his attention focused on his daughter, with her light-colored hair and dark shirt.

He leaned forward, bracing his hands against the desk, watching Harper run toward the swings.

"Wait, what's that?" Sky pointed at a dark shape outside the chain-link fence. The shape hovered in and out of view as if moving between the bushes as it worked its way around to the back of the playground.

"Somebody's there," he said grimly.

Ms. Breton frowned. "The teachers must not have noticed."

As they watched, the shape vanished and didn't appear again. Then Harper skipped along beside the fence, pausing for a moment near a cluster of bushes that stood on the other side. She went running over to the side of the building, beyond the camera's range. Bode's heart lurched when she didn't reappear.

"Where did she go?" Sky clutched her hands together. Ms. Breton kept the video playing as the children lined up again and followed the teachers back inside.

All of them but Harper.

"Mr. Tucker, someone cut the fence to let her out. We

found the damage after reviewing the footage, just before you arrived."

Bode gritted his teeth so hard his jaw ached. Never had he thought his job would put Harper in danger. "Show me." He and Sky followed the director out a side door leading directly onto the playground, stopping in front of the section where Harper had vanished off the camera feed. Bushes obscured the chain-link fence in this area, and he had to wedge his shoulders into the foliage and stoop to examine it. His heart sank when his gaze landed on a section that had been snipped and pulled back. The opening was just big enough to let a three-year-old out.

Bode stood again, gesturing at the fence. "Why wasn't someone paying attention?" The words came out in a harsh bark, as if asking could somehow undo what had happened. But deep down, he knew it wasn't the school's fault. How could they anticipate a criminal coming after his daughter?

"I'm so sorry," the director said. "You can be assured we'll discuss this incident with our staff and look for ways to improve security." She wrung her hands. "We've never had anything like this happen before."

And why would Harper have left at all? He dragged a hand through his hair. "She knows better than to go anywhere with a stranger. Why would she do that?"

Sky's eyes glistened with moisture. "Maybe he told her he would take her to see you. Or that you were hurt and needed her."

His throat burned but he nodded, then pulled out his phone. Sky shot him a questioning look. "I'm calling the tip line."

The killer wasn't after Harper; he was after Sky. And possibly Bode now, too. With the way he'd been toying with them, maybe he'd left a clue. Bode tapped through to the voice mail system, then entered his access code. In the distance, thunder rumbled as the storm front rolled closer. Tension gripped his ribs.

"One new message," the automated voice said, "from anonymous."

He pressed Play, then put it on speaker phone. "Track the cell phone." The male voice was garbled, like it had been run through some sort of filter. He hung up, then glanced at Sky.

Her eyes went wide. "He means mine, doesn't he? The one I dropped?"

"I think so." *Please, God, let my little girl be okay.* He turned to the director. "Ms. Breton, please keep everyone off the playground until law enforcement arrives to check for evidence. We need to go now."

He tossed his keys to Sky as they jogged to the parking lot. "You drive. I'll call the chief ranger to update him. But first we're going to track your phone again."

They climbed into the vehicle, and he handed her his phone after unlocking it. She typed in her account information and waited for the page to load.

"Come on..." he muttered. Now wasn't the time for the park's sketchy cell service to die, and in his rush to get to Harper, he'd left his two-way radio back at headquarters.

"Here, take it." She pushed the phone into his hands. "I'll get the car started."

Finally, a map appeared. Unlike the other times they'd checked, now a bright green dot flashed on the screen. "Got it." He zoomed in, then took a screenshot of the location in case they lost service before he could get there. "Take a right out of the lot and go west. We're heading toward Yosemite Falls. The ping is coming from about halfway between Camp 4 and the base of the falls."

Thunder rumbled again, closer this time. A bank of dark clouds filled the skyline in front of them, towering high above the Valley. The park's usual traffic overload had converged onto the main roads exiting the Valley as visitors tried to leave before the storm hit. He pulled up Chief Kleinman in his contacts and hit the call button. The ringtone stuttered in and out of his hearing as his service wobbled. When the call went to voice mail, he left a brief message explaining that Harper had been taken and that he and Sky were going after her. "About halfway between Yosemite Falls and the falls trailhead. I'll text the screensh—"

The call cut out. He groaned, watching the signal icon for more bars to appear, but he had nothing.

"What?" Sky asked. The first drops of rain sprinkled the windshield.

"I lost service." After attaching the screenshot to a text, he hit Send, just in case it had the chance to get through.

Her throat bobbed, but she nodded. Was she afraid?

"You can stay with the car, if you'd feel better. I know it's not…" *Great out here. What you signed up for. What any of us wanted.* He bit his tongue. Negativity wouldn't help them recover his daughter.

"No way. I'm not leaving you to look for her alone." She bit her lip, as if she'd wanted to say more, but instead she flipped on the windshield wipers.

"Take that side road." He jabbed a finger out the passenger window. "It'll get us closer to where we need to be." And out of the traffic. Dust flew up in a cloud as the car bounced onto an unpaved road. Soon the rain would turn it into mud, but the drops weren't coming fast enough yet. Still only a sprinkle.

Lightning streaked in the distance, followed by a loud boom a few seconds later. Her knuckles were white around the wheel, and her throat bobbed again. Did she feel like she had to come with him? She wasn't used to being out here in the wilderness with a storm bearing down. Had he pressured her in some way?

"Hey, if you don't feel comfortable—"

"Bode. I'm coming with you." Steel lined her tone, warning him he hadn't given her enough credit. "I'm not afraid for myself. I'm worried about Harper. She must be terrified."

"She hates storms." He balled a hand into a fist, then forced it to unclench. "Thanks, Sky. I…" *I'm so glad I'm not alone right now. I need your strength.* But he couldn't say that, couldn't follow that train of thought where it might lead. "I appreciate you being here."

She reached over, squeezed his hand tightly and released it. Warmth unfurled in his chest, somehow soothing and uncomfortable at the same time.

He leaned forward to study the cliff walls rising ahead of them, then glanced back at the screenshot he'd taken. Still no cell service. The storm must be interfering with it. He'd have to direct them without the benefit of GPS tracking. At least the storm had cleared out all the visitors from this part of the Valley.

"There." He pointed to a gravel turnout that visitors sometimes used for overflow parking. It was empty now. "Park there. We'll have to go the rest of the way on foot."

She pulled in and shut off the engine, then handed him the keys.

"Sorry about the rain." He opened his door. With the way the wind was picking up, they didn't have long before a full-on downpour began.

"That's okay, I won't melt." She climbed out and shut her door, then trotted around to his side. The wind whipped at her long red hair, and she struggled to gather it into a ponytail.

"This way." He pointed toward the cliff walls rising over the forest then took off in a slow jog with Sky at his heels.

When they entered the cover of the trees, the rain pattered on the leaves far overhead. He slowed his pace. Now that he had a plan, now that he was taking steps to get to his daughter, a nagging thought had worked its way up from his subconscious. The killer had masterminded this plan, taking Sky's phone and then abducting Harper. There was only one reason he could think of: to get to him and Sky.

Were they walking into a trap?

Sky kept close to Bode's side as they jogged through the woods, dodging exposed roots and rocks and avoiding trees. Thunder rumbled overhead, but the rain wasn't falling hard enough yet to reach them through the canopy.

Hairs prickled on the back of her neck the deeper they got into the woods. What if this was all a trick? What if Harper wasn't out here at all, and the killer was just trying to lure her and Bode into the open?

Then again, maybe it didn't matter. After all, it was *her* fault Harper was in danger. If Bode hadn't gotten stuck with her case, he and Harper would never have been thrust into the killer's spotlight.

The sky had grown ominously dark in the last few minutes, made worse by the deep shadows beneath the trees. Rain hammered the canopy above, dripping down in giant drops that splattered the tops of her head and shoulders. Lightning flickered, and thunder clapped so close she nearly jumped out of her skin.

Bode glanced back at her. "You all right?"

She nodded mutely.

"We're almost there. Once we get through the trees, we'll be able to see along the cliff base to where your phone was pinging." His Adam's apple bobbed, and she longed to reach for him to comfort him.

I'm so sorry I put you in this position. The words were right there, but now wasn't the time, not when the focus needed to be on Harper.

Minutes later, they reached the edge of the tree line. Wind whipped across their faces, tearing strands of hair loose from her ponytail and pelting her with cold rain. She edged closer to Bode, scanning the nearby landscape for any sign of movement.

"Do you see anything?" She had to yell to be heard over the storm.

"No." He swiped rain from his face and flicked the water off his hands in quick, brusque motions. "I have to go out there. You stay here, beneath the cover of the trees."

She grabbed his arm before he could take off. "I'm coming with you."

"Sky." He pivoted to face her. "We could be running into a trap."

"I know. But it's my fault Harper is in danger. I'm going to do whatever I can to help make sure she's safe."

A muscle ticked in his jaw. "It's *not* your fault. But there's no time to argue. Come on."

He dashed out from beneath the cover of the trees, and she raced after him before he could vanish into the elements. Cold water pummeled her in sheets, biting through her uniform.

She kept close to Bode as he crossed the open terrain between the woods and the valley wall. As he approached the cliff, he veered to the right, heading along the base in the direction of Yosemite Falls. Her lungs ached and her sodden shirt clung to her back as she followed him. Each crash of thunder sent her heart up into her throat.

Then they rounded a bend, and a small, dark shape came into view against the light-colored granite. *Harper?*

Bode dashed ahead while Sky jogged after him. She scanned the perimeter, but there was no sign of anyone else within her limited visibility. Just pouring rain and green grass before the world dissolved into an amorphous haze.

Then Bode crashed to his knees ahead of her and pulled the dark shape up onto his lap. Was she still alive?

Seconds later she reached the two of them, dropping to the soaked ground next to Bode. Harper's blond hair matted her pale face, but her eyes were open, her teeth chattering. "Daddy," she stuttered. Her little chest lifted and fell with regular breaths above her hands, which had been tied together in front of her stomach.

Thank You, Lord! Relief crashed through Sky's chest.

Bode pulled out a pocketknife from his utility belt. "Harper, honey, I'm going to get these ropes off you. Hold still for me, baby."

Sky crawled around to her other side, rubbing a hand reassuringly against the little girl's back. "Harper, I'm so glad to see you again."

"Hi, Miss Skylar." Harper turned to her, a smile lighting up her face despite everything. Warmth filled Sky's chest. "Me no like this rain."

"Me either." Relief made laughter gurgle in her chest, and she glanced up at Bode. The look on his face nearly wrecked her—the intensity of his love for his daughter. He smiled, but she felt sure those were tears streaming down his cheeks, mixed with the rain. To see a man as strong as he was weep over nearly losing his child did something to her insides. A beautiful earthly picture of the way God loved His children, too.

After he'd cut through the ropes, he twisted Harper around on his lap. "Miss Skylar, can you help me check Harper for injuries?"

"Of course." She peered into Harper's eyes, turning her head one way and then the other. When she bopped the child on the nose, the little girl giggled. "Does anything hurt?" She touched her arms and legs, but nothing felt amiss, and there were no visible wounds besides chafing on her skin from the rope.

"No. Better now."

Bode's eyes closed for a moment as he hugged her tightly, then kissed the top of her head. "I'm better now, too. Let's get out of this rain." He swiped his cheeks, then looked at Sky. "Any sign of…?"

She shook her head. "But the visibility is terrible." An idea occurred to her. "What about my phone?"

"Right, I forgot about that. Check the ground?"

She checked the area along the cliff base where Harper had been lying. There—a small black rectangle lying half-buried in the grass. "Found it." After wiping off as much water and mud as she could, she tucked it into a pocket of her soaked pants. "But if he's not out here, what was the point?"

"I don't know." He shook his head. "It doesn't make—"

A boom cracked overhead, brief and sharp like a gunshot but deeper. Not thunder. Sky looked up, searching for the source, just in time to catch a burst of flame projecting out from the cliff face. Almost like— "Was that an explosion?"

Bode craned his neck, staring upward. The boom echoed off the cliffs until it was overtaken by loud rumbling.

Harper covered her ears, shrinking deeper into Bode's lap, and fear skittered along Sky's arms.

What *was* that?

Then suddenly Bode shoved Harper toward her. "Rockfall. Take her. Go!"

She scooped Harper up and raced along the cliff face. The rain had eased, but the bellowing overhead sounded closer. Dust filled the air, and small pebbles pelted her face. She didn't dare turn back to look for Bode. Harper clung to her arms, bouncing against her hip as she ran.

But the child was heavy, and Sky's legs and arms ached. How much farther to get beyond the danger? Then she spied an overhang up ahead, forming an alcove beneath it. If it was deep enough, maybe it would provide the protection they needed.

"Run!" Bode huffed from behind, his voice barely audible over the roar coming down the mountainside.

She dared a glance up and instantly regretted it. A wall of rock and debris rushed down the cliff face like a ceiling ready to collapse on them. They'd be crushed instantly. And her legs felt like jelly.

Her breath came in great gasps. Fire seared her muscles.

Only a few more steps…

But the leading edge of the rockslide was almost upon them. A second or two, at the most, was all she had.

They weren't going to make it.

NINE

Sky braced for impact, pressing Harper to her chest. The rocks would slam down on her any second.

Then a different force shoved her from behind, and she stumbled forward under the overhang. *Bode?* She screamed his name, but the sound was lost in the deafening crash of rocks cascading around her. Retreating to the deepest part of the alcove, she pressed her back against solid rock. Harper crammed her face into Sky's shoulder, pinching her arms as she clung on for dear life. A cloud of dust filled the space, making them both cough.

But where was Bode? He'd been right behind her, close enough to shove her to safety. Had he made it?

Panic gripped her chest, squeezing so hard her ribs felt like they might crack. Harper needed him. *She* needed him.

The thunderous roll stopped within seconds, until only isolated rocks could be heard smashing to the ground nearby. She waved dust away from their faces and helped Harper pull her shirt up over her mouth.

"Bode?" She blinked away grit, straining to see in the shadowy space. The rockslide had fully covered almost the entire alcove, leaving only a thin stream of light illuminating a shaft of dust. She pushed away from the back wall and stumbled forward, clinging tightly to Harper.

Then she spied his green uniform pants where he lay curled on his side barely a foot away from the mound of debris. She carried Harper to him and got down on her knees.

"Harper, sit here next to me, okay? We need to check on your daddy."

"Daddy?" The little girl patted his shoulder, and when he didn't stir, a sob nearly ripped out of Sky's chest. If she'd been the cause of his death, if she'd cost Harper another parent…

An answering groan made her heart spasm. "Bode? Don't move yet, okay? I need to see where you're injured."

He rolled onto his back, fully ignoring her instructions, then pushed himself up into a seated position. "Are you and Harper all right?"

"Yes." Her voice came out thick around a mouthful of *what-ifs*. "We're okay, thanks to you." He'd saved her yet again. She couldn't keep putting him and Harper in danger like this.

"Daddy." Harper started to crawl onto his lap, but Sky pulled her back.

"Wait a minute, sweetheart. We need to make sure he isn't hurt." She scanned his face, noting a trickle of blood from his forehead. "You're bleeding." She looked around for anything clean she could press to the wound, then settled for ripping off one of her shirt sleeves. An amused expression flitted across his features as she pressed the fabric to the cut. "What?"

"You're violating dress code, Ranger. I may have to write you up."

"Next time I'll let you treat your own wounds," she teased. Even in the shadowy darkness, she could see light dancing in his eyes. An impulsive urge swept over her to touch his face, to feel the rough stubble of his cheeks beneath her fingertips, but she forced her attention to the wound on his forehead. “Any other injuries? Were you struck?”

He reached for his shoulder, and she pulled her hand back as he felt along it, then rotated it. “I took a hit to my shoulder, but it seems to be okay. Bruises but nothing broken. How about you?”

“Fine, thanks to you. What about you, Harper? Are you okay?” She held the little girl out from her, scanning her for any sign of injury. Harper stared back at her with big hazel eyes and nodded.

“Come here, sweet pea.” Bode opened his arms, and the little girl climbed into his lap. He kissed the top of her head.

She clapped her chubby little hands together, creating clouds of dust. Amazing how resilient kids were, although Harper would have a lot to process after what she'd gone through. *Thank You, Lord, for giving her Bode as a father.* “Me dirty, Daddy. Go home?”

“That is an excellent idea.” He glanced around the alcove, more of a cave now thanks to the rockfall. “How big is that opening?”

Sky scrambled to her feet and picked her way over, careful of the rocks scattered across the ground. The hole was close to her height, and she stepped up onto a fallen rock to get a better look, mindful not to hit her head on the ceiling created by the overhang. This close to the outside world, she felt a blast of cold wind and rain hit her face.

“Harper could squeeze through. I might be able to.” Not Bode though, with his broad shoulders. “We'd have to move some of this to get you out.”

“Wait here, sweet pea.” He set Harper down and walked over, stopping next to Sky.

She glanced up, reminded again of how much taller he

was. He peered out, watching the pelting rain splatter on the fallen rock outside their cave. Thunder growled again in the distance, and the sky had grown even darker as the sun slid toward the west. "Wait, what's that?"

She followed the line where he was pointing to a dark shape picking its way across the debris from the rockfall. Every cell in her body froze. "That's not help already, is it?" Was it *him*? The killer?

"No." His voice was low and soft. "That's not help. Not yet. I texted our approximate location to Chief Kleinman earlier, but there's no way anyone got out here this fast. Get back against the wall with Harper."

She did as he said, taking Harper in her arms and pressing her back against the cold wall. Bode pulled his gun from its holster and angled his body closer to the edge of their small peephole.

"Daddy?" Harper's little voice split the silence in the cave, sending a jolt of adrenaline zipping through Sky's system. Bode shook his head.

"Shhh," she urged, whispering into Harper's hair. "We have to be very quiet right now." Hopefully the rain and wind outside would be enough to stop the sound of her voice from carrying.

The little girl nodded against her, burying her face in Sky's neck. She watched Bode over the top of Harper's head. He stood still as a statue, gun up, finger on the trigger. Watching and waiting.

After what felt like an eternity, his posture relaxed. He stuffed the gun back into its holster and walked over to her and Harper, pulling the two of them into an unexpected embrace. At the warmth and security of his touch, Sky's legs wobbled.

"Shh, it's okay. He's gone." He pressed her close for

a moment, then released her and held out his hands for Harper. “Here, let me take her.”

“What happened?” She slid down to the ground, grateful to sit before her legs gave out. “Was he looking for us?”

In the fading light, Bode nodded. He took a seat next to her, settling Harper into his lap. “Yes. He came right up to the base of the rocks and stood there for a minute, as if listening for us. Then kept going. He must’ve triggered the rockfall with an explosive.”

“After luring us out here.” A shudder rippled through her back. “What do we do now?”

“I think it’s best if we wait here. Let him think we didn’t make it. The chief ranger will get someone out here as soon as he can.”

“Daddy?” Harper’s voice wobbled. “Me wanna go home. Get Leepop.”

“I know, baby,” he said into her hair. “But we’re gonna have a little campout here tonight instead. Lollipop will watch our house for us.” He turned to Sky. “That’s her favorite stuffy.” Then back to Harper. “Some good men from Daddy’s work will come and help us get out soon.”

“Okay, Daddy.”

Bode stroked the little girl’s hair gently. “Sweet pea, what happened at school today? Why did you leave the playground with a stranger?”

Sky shivered. They’d come so close to losing Harper completely. When they escaped this cave, she’d tell Bode he needed to hand her case off to someone else. Or maybe she should leave Yosemite altogether.

“He was your friend, Daddy. He said we’d see you.”

And he *had* taken Harper to Bode…in a really twisted, evil way. Her gaze found Bode’s, and the fear that flashed in his eyes mirrored how she felt.

"No like him." Harper sniffled. "Not friend."

"No, he isn't my friend, but God worked it out. You're safe with me and Miss Skylar now," Bode soothed. "But that's why you can't go anywhere with strangers. Because you can't tell when they're lying."

"Is bad to lie." The little girl nodded.

"Yes, it is," Sky confirmed. "But sometimes bad guys will do it anyway to trick you. Like the bad man did today."

"You need to stay with your teachers next time, Harper. You can tell them if someone tries to get you to leave. Nobody knew where you were." He squeezed her tighter, and his eyes glistened in the fading light.

"Jesus took care of us today. He's our friend, and He's always with us." Sky reached over and placed a hand gently on his arm before pulling away. She longed to comfort him, but it wasn't her place, not when they were only colleagues. Maybe they could even become friends, but nothing more. The thought stung far more than it should. When had this man—and his sweet little daughter—worked their way so deep into her heart?

"Yes, He is. He'll never leave nor forsake us." Bode smiled at her. Even with the dirt smudging his cheeks and dusting his messy hair, her heart did funny flips in her chest.

She cleared her throat, forcing her attention away from his blue eyes and onto Harper. "Harper, you like princesses, right? Who's your favorite?"

Hopefully having something she liked to talk about would help soothe the child after her distressing ordeal. She'd gone through far more than anyone her age should have to face. The little girl chattered for several minutes as Sky asked questions. Bode tipped his head back, his shoulders slumping as he relaxed. It made Sky happy to see him comfortable, knowing she could help in this small way. Even now, he must be so scared for his daughter. When Harper asked Sky to tell a story, she launched into an animated recounting of *The Princess and the Pea.*

When she finished, Harper giggled. "Me want pea under my bed."

Sky laughed, glancing at Bode. His eyes were shut, his breathing steady. "I'll tell your daddy when he wakes up."

"I'm awake," he mumbled, without opening his eyes. "Barely."

She and Harper giggled again.

"Miss Skylar sing?" Harper nestled deeper into Bode's lap, resting her head against his chest. He dragged one of his arms up tighter around her. "Daddy's not very good."

"Nobody speaks the truth like a three-year-old." Bode rolled his head her direction, pried his eyes open and winked. "Isla had a beautiful voice."

No pressure, Skylar. She almost said no, but this request wasn't about her or impressing Bode. It was about comforting Harper during an awful situation. So she cleared her throat, then began one of her favorite hymns. *"Be thou my vision, O Lord of my heart. Naught be all else to me, save that Thou art..."*

She closed her eyes, drinking in the simple comfort of the words. How long it had been since she'd felt so close to her Savior. Out here, she'd faced the worst physical trials—and fear—of her life, and yet she'd never felt so secure. Both because of the Lord's steadfast presence and because He'd used this man next to her to protect her time and again.

The last strains of the song echoed gently around them. Harper's breaths came in a slow, steady rhythm, and her eyes were closed. Sky glanced up at Bode, half-afraid to read his opinion of her singing on his face, but found herself trapped in a tender blue gaze. He studied her, his lips parted just slightly.

Her insides melted like chocolate in a double boiler, and she leaned closer to him until their shoulders brushed.

His Adam's apple bobbed, and he looked down at his daughter. "Thank you," he whispered. "She's asleep."

Right, *of course*—he was thinking about Harper, not her. She shook herself out of her stupor and stared down at her hands. Her chest deflated like a burst balloon, swiftly followed by a kick of annoyance at herself for feeling that way. "Sure," she said casually, straightening her back to put some space between them.

He cleared his throat. "Sorry you're stuck out here overnight. I'm sure this isn't what you were hoping for when you signed up to work in Yosemite."

His words brought her back full force to their precarious situation. Guilt swelled in her stomach. "No, *I'm* sorry. If it weren't for me, Harper wouldn't be in danger." She dragged her hands over her face. "I should leave as soon as we get out of here. If anything more happened to her…" Her eyes burned. "I can't let that be my fault."

She just couldn't. Her family had fallen apart when her father had vanished, and yet Bode and Harper had managed to survive the loss of his wife. She couldn't take that away from him. And if there was one thing she learned from Chris, it was to recognize her own inadequacy. She couldn't keep Harper safe. She couldn't keep Bode out of harm's way either. In fact, all she was doing was making things worse.

Leaving would be the best option, no matter how much it would hurt to say goodbye. Her employment was up at the end of the summer. It was better to go now, get it over with and keep Harper safe.

* * *

Bode tightened his arms around Harper, letting loose a soul-deep sigh of relief. He'd come way too close to losing her. After Isla, he wasn't sure he could take another hit to his heart like that. And they weren't out of the woods yet. Even once they got back, there'd be statements to give and the school to contact. The sheriff's department might want to interview Harper. How would his little girl handle all the questions? He hated for her to relive all the trauma over again. Then he'd need to talk to Ms. Breton and possibly the school's board about increasing the security measures. Preventing anything like this from happening again.

Somewhere in the midst of his racing thoughts, Sky's soft words hit home. *I should leave as soon as we get out of here.* Yet another loss heading his way, one that mattered to him far more than it should. Yet Sky shouldn't be blaming herself for what had happened to Harper. There was nothing she could've done to prevent this situation.

"Skylar." Her name rasped from his lips in a harsh whisper, which made her look up. The sorrow buried in her eyes twisted through his insides. How could he reassure her? "This is not your fault. It's my job to tackle these kinds of cases. *I'm* the one risking Harper's safety, not you." He kissed Harper softly on the top of the head. "And believe me, I feel awful about it. My sister has tried to get me to leave Harper with her, but… I can't. Not when she's all I have left."

Maybe he should listen to her. What was stopping the next perp from targeting his family? And yet, he couldn't leave his job, not when God had called him to protect the innocent and find justice for those who had been harmed.

He glanced at Sky to find her watching him. Her eyes glistened, and she blinked.

"How did you get through it? When your wife passed? What happened with Chris nearly wrecked me, and it was just a breakup. With a man who wasn't even all that great. And my mom..." She wrapped her arms over her chest. "When Dad disappeared, it was like we lost her, too. In a way, I became Addie's parent. How have you...?"

Stayed sane? Made his feet get out of bed each morning? He smiled, reaching over to take one of her small hands in his. She had a sensitive, empathetic heart, and he admired how much she cared.

"It was touch and go for a while, I'll be honest. I think I told you before how Reese and the team helped keep me going, but ultimately it was the Lord. Every morning I'd wake up and see His goodness and grace in Harper and in all the little things. And in my memories with Isla. I'd still do it all again, even knowing how it ended."

"That's a beautiful testimony. I wouldn't trade my years with my dad either." She squeezed his hand, then pulled away, swiping her cheeks. "Though I can't say the same about my relationship with my ex-boyfriend."

Thoughts swirled in his brain, trying to congeal into words like freshly poured Jell-O. One thing stood out above them all: she deserved all the love a man had to offer. "I don't want to overstep my bounds, like I might've on the trail this morning, but whatever happened between you and Chris... He didn't deserve you. We haven't known each other long, but I can assure you that you are beautiful, inside and out. Strong, courageous, kind, concerned about others even when you have every right to be selfish. Your faith has held steady through all the horrible things you've endured. And..."

The words died out as he stared into her soft eyes, more gray than green in the dying light. An invisible force pulled him closer to her as warmth spiraled through his chest. Here she was, covered in dust and grime, and so different than Isla—yet so undeniably beautiful. He hadn't thought he'd ever feel this magnetic pull toward another woman again, and yet here he was, caught in Skylar's orbit like an asteroid that couldn't escape. What would it feel like, to kiss those soft lips? Her eyes widened a fraction, and the air crackled between them as the gap shrank.

Then Harper twitched, crying out in her sleep, and Bode jerked back like he'd been about to kiss a hot iron. Had he taken total leave of his senses?

"I..." Whatever he was going to say vanished in a haze of longing and regret.

Sky shifted next to him. She was barely visible now in the dying light. Soon they'd be consumed by total darkness. "Is she still asleep?"

"Yeah, she's fine."

She was giving him an out, the chance to pretend like that almost-kiss hadn't happened. But they'd both remember, and it would hang like a cloud over their working relationship. As much as he'd rather not, he needed to take the lead and address the situation before things got more awkward.

"Sky..." He paused, trying to find the right words. When had talking turned into such a challenge?

"Bode, it's okay." She made a sound as if rubbing her arms. "We have a case to solve, and that's what matters. I'll probably think about moving on after this season, anyway. I only came out here to get away from Chris and the stress of my old life. It wasn't meant to be permanent." Her voice dropped. "You don't owe me anything."

He wished he could wrap an arm around her and pull her close, but doing so would be the exact opposite of what they both needed. Still, he felt obliged to explain. "I have to think about Harper. I can't put her through losing anyone else important to her."

He couldn't do it to himself either, if he were being honest. He'd survived the past few years—but barely. Another loss like that might break him. Yes, the thought of Sky moving away stung more than he wanted it to, but he'd only known her for a few days. He'd get over these unruly feelings.

Right?

"Of course. You don't need to explain." She adjusted her position next to him. "Any luck with the cell service?"

Well, good to know she wasn't hurt. Or disappointed. Maybe she wasn't as emotionally invested as he was. He swallowed down the burning in his throat and checked his phone, which he'd set on the ground next to him. "Nothing. Why don't you try to get some sleep, and I'll keep checking?"

She mumbled something, then grew silent. He almost offered to let her lean against him, but after the conversation they'd just had, it felt too pushy. Or too contradictory, maybe. So instead he tipped his head back against the cold rocks and hugged Harper closer, trying to ignore the loneliness clawing at his chest.

TEN

Sky slept fitfully, shifting every time her backside grew too sore or her legs too stiff. Sometime in the night the storm had passed, leaving cold air in its wake. And even when her body grew too exhausted to fight sleep, her brain—and heart—wouldn't cooperate. She kept turning that near kiss, and the conversation afterward, over in her mind. How Bode had offered a half apology, half explanation, and how she'd wanted to do the same. But at the exact same time she'd wanted to throw caution to the wind and kiss the man like tomorrow would never come.

She roused to the sound of a bird chirping outside. Faint light trickled in through the opening in their cave. Her neck ached something fierce, but delicious warmth radiated against her cheek and left side, making up just a little for the goose bumps popping on her arms and legs. When she lifted her head, she realized why. Sometime in the night she'd fallen asleep on Bode's shoulder. He was still out, head tilted back against the wall, eyes sealed shut.

Harper lay sandwiched between their legs on the cold ground, her head in Bode's lap. Her eyes flicked open when Sky shifted.

"Miss Skylar." Harper reached chubby fingers up toward Sky's face. Sky caught her hand and squeezed.

"How'd you like your first campout in a cave?"

"Bad. But me like you and Daddy." She pulled her hand loose and waved it over her head, near Bode's face. He grunted, shifting slightly, but stayed asleep.

"I like you and your daddy, too." A lot. More than she should, given their awkward "define the relationship" talk or whatever that was last night. Her moving on from Yosemite was probably going to be the best call for all of them.

When Harper succeeded in batting him in the chin, Bode startled awake. "What are you doing, little munchkin?"

"Wake up, Daddy! Me want breakfast."

As if on cue, his stomach grumbled. "I guess I do, too."

Sky laughed. "That makes three of us. Wait—" She sat up, listening. It had almost sounded like someone was calling their names.

"I heard it, too. Somebody's there." He moved Harper off his lap, scrambled to his feet then walked over to the opening. After listening for a moment, he cupped his hands around his mouth and leaned into the hole. "Over here!"

"Daddy?" Harper glanced between Sky and Bode's back.

Sky stood, holding her hands out to Harper. "Come here. I'll hold you. They're coming to rescue us."

The little girl stepped into her arms, and she settled Harper onto her hip then walked over to stand near Bode. Minutes later a flashlight shone into the hole, making them all blink.

"They're here!" a man called.

Another face flashed before the hole—the deputy assigned to be her roommate. "Rachel!" Relief surged through Sky. She'd trusted they would get out of here alive, but after everything she'd endured the past few days, she knew better than to take rescue for granted.

"Great to see you, Deputy Moore," Bode said.

"We'll get you out of there in a jiffy." She pointed at Sky. "Don't go vanishing on me like that again."

"Yes, ma'am." Sky gave a mock salute.

"I'll make sure she doesn't." Bode laughed, wrapping his arm around her shoulders. Warmth seared her insides, and she couldn't help noticing how neatly she fit against him. But then he released her, stuffing his hand into his pocket.

When Chief Kleinman arrived a few minutes later, puffing and out of breath, he and Bode began a protracted conversation about the safest way to extract them. Finally, it was decided the three of them should press back against the wall, where the natural overhang would offer protection, as the others removed enough debris to allow them out.

An hour later, she scrambled out into a bright, sparkling morning. Bode handed Harper up to her, then crawled out after. The sky was a brilliant sapphire blue dotted with cotton ball clouds, and the rain had left drops of water shining like diamonds on every leaf and blade of grass.

She inhaled a deep breath of damp, morning air and exhaled a silent prayer of gratitude. They'd found Harper, the overhang had been right where they needed it and help had arrived before the killer realized they weren't actually dead. If that wasn't God's faithfulness, Sky didn't know what was.

Her gaze landed on Bode, who was covered head to toe in dirt, and she smothered a smile beneath her hand as he looked her way.

"What are you laughing at?" He nudged her with his elbow as they walked with their escort back to waiting vehicles. Harper clung to him on one side as he carried her close.

"You look like a coal miner with all that dirt."

"Hey, you're no spa client either, you know."

They both laughed, then Harper joined in, giggling even though she probably had no idea why. Warmth radiated from Bode's eyes as he glanced at Sky over the top of the little girl's head.

Half an hour later they were back at park headquarters in the ISB conference room. One of the staff had purchased some breakfast for them, and Harper dove into her scrambled eggs and bowl of Froot Loops like she hadn't eaten in weeks. The little girl had been quite the trouper.

Over breakfast, they gave Chief Kleinman a brief rundown of the previous night's events, and Bode had even managed to coax Harper into retelling as much as she could about what had happened at the daycare center.

Kleinman jotted down notes, then glanced up. "I'll get a team out to search the site for evidence of the explosion. We'll keep the area closed off to visitors as well, until we can deem it safe. I've already handed the abduction case to the sheriff's office. I imagine they'll be in touch soon."

"Thank you, Chief." Bode had shoveled in two breakfast burritos almost faster than Sky could blink. She'd been starved, too, but now that it was time to consider their next move, her appetite had all but died. "I need to get Harper home—" he glanced first at her, then at Harper tucked between them "—and then I'm going to see about taking her down to my sister's. After what happened, I'd feel better knowing she's safe."

His words hit her like a ton of granite as her thoughts from last night came crashing back in. "Chief, Agent Tucker, would it help if I leave the area? Maybe you'd be able to conduct the investigation without all these incidents."

"No," Bode objected, "that wouldn't help. The killer might come after you, leaving you in danger and making him harder for us to catch. Or if he lets you leave, he might vanish."

She let out a slow sigh, looking to the chief and Rachel. They both nodded.

"We can protect you much easier if you're here," Rachel said.

Their reasoning did nothing to assuage her guilt, but she smoothed back her hair and didn't argue. "That's fair."

She looked at Bode, trying to read his thoughts. Did he want her to go with him to his sister's? Should she offer? Or would that be pushing the boundaries of their professional relationship?

Chief Kleinman snapped his fingers. "Before I forget, a visitor found a handgun in the woods half a mile from the clearing this morning. A member of their party reported the location at the nearest station."

Bode straightened. "Could be from our killer. That's great news."

The chief nodded. "I sent someone out to retrieve it." He patted the armrests on his chair then stood. "We'll keep you posted on both that and the rockfall investigation."

Bode rose and shook the chief's hand, and Sky leaned down to Harper. "You ready to go home?"

Harper nodded, then reached for her, climbing into her lap. "Miss Sky come, too?"

Sky wrapped her arms around the little girl, pressing her cheek against the soft blond hair. "I don't know, but I hope so."

The conference room grew quiet, and when she looked up, only Bode and Rachel were left. Rachel was occupied typing something on her phone, but Bode had his gaze locked on Sky and Harper, and the longing that flashed through his eyes nearly stole her breath. Then he blinked and crouched down next to them.

"Maybe this is asking too much—" he fidgeted with a

loose thread on his shirt "—but would you mind coming with me and Harper?" His brows lifted, and the hopefulness in his eyes made her feel like floating. He cleared his throat. "I mean, my sister lives in Fresno, so we could track down that friend of Jeremy Flint's. Scott Simmons?"

Right, of course—the case. That was all he was thinking about. "Yeah, that sounds like a good plan. I can come."

Harper clapped her hands then grabbed Sky's to clap with her. Sky laughed, aware that her chest felt suddenly lighter.

Rachel pocketed her phone. "Unless you need me to tag along, I'll stay here and help with the investigation. And make sure the killer doesn't attempt to break into your lodgings, Skylar."

"And that will help maintain the illusion you're still here," Bode added, looking at her. "Do you want to grab an overnight bag? We might need to crash at my sister's place tonight. It's a two-and-a-half-hour drive."

She nodded. "Good idea."

"I'll call my sister while we're waiting for you." He took a few minutes to pack his laptop and notes from his desk, then drove Sky and Harper back to Sky's apartment. Rachel followed in her vehicle, sticking close until Sky was safely back in Bode's car with an overnight bag.

She and Bode waved goodbye to the deputy, and he started the engine.

"Chelsea said she'd love to take Harper while we wrap up this case, and we can stay at her place overnight." Bode steered out onto the main road that would take them out of the Valley. "I also tracked down the most recent address on record for Scott Simmons, so we can pay him a visit this afternoon."

"Good. I'm wondering if he can tell us more about the

EMT, Kathryn, and her connection to Jeremy Flint. She vanished after my father did, which makes me wonder if she knew about Jeremy's—" she glanced into the back seat, where Harper sang to herself as she played with a doll "—*activities* and either was an accomplice or became a victim. If she were obsessed enough, she might even be driven to revenge."

He glanced at her. "But you feel confident it was a man after you in the clearing?"

"Yes." She chewed the inside of her lip. "I can't shake the feeling though that we're missing some connection. If Jeremy did survive that fall, how could he be lurking around the park, not getting caught?"

"New name and identity? Or plastic surgery." He winced. "That could make it even harder to identify him."

"Or maybe it's not him at all. Just someone with his height and build who wants revenge on his behalf." She stared out the window at the gorgeous scenery rolling past, wishing she could see the answer painted across one of the granite cliff faces.

"I'd say his brother Steven, but his record is spotless. And given that he knew about Jeremy's history with the law and was there for the accident, I just don't see the motive." Bode slowed the vehicle as they exited the park past a ranger station then accelerated again.

After a few miles he pointed to a road on the right. "Yosemite Mountaineering School, where I worked before I took my job with the park service, is up that way. And now we're almost to El Portal." He tightened his grip on the wheel, then relaxed his fingers. "I keep forgetting you grew up here. Where did you live when your father worked here?"

"We had a home in Wawona, in the south. Mom worked

at a lodge down there. She loved the quaint charm of the place."

He turned off the highway onto a side road that took them past older ranches and small log cabins. A sign ahead announced they were approaching National Park Service housing, and Bode slowed his speed.

"Here's home. Isla always wanted to buy our own place, but as you can probably tell, housing out here is limited and *very* expensive." He drove past a stretch of duplexes before turning onto a cul-de-sac lined with small bungalows that looked exactly like the government housing she remembered. Neutral exterior paint, identical facades, minimal landscaping.

"Yay, home!" Harper clapped from the back seat. "See, Miss Sky?" She jammed a chubby finger at the window.

Bode turned into the driveway, which ended in a carport attached to the house. They climbed out of the car, and she followed a pace behind him as he carried Harper. He'd lived here with his wife. Stayed after she passed. And now he was bringing *her* here, just temporarily, but… Did it feel strange to him? Had he brought any other women here? Given the little she knew of him, she highly doubted it.

He unlocked the door, stepped inside with Harper and held it open for her. She paused on the threshold, surveying the linoleum and industrial carpet. Farther in, she caught a glimpse of cozy plaid furniture and a bookcase lined with books and photographs. Baskets of toys filled a low shelf.

She hadn't been in a man's home in a long time, not since the last dinner party Chris had held in his luxurious apartment. Somehow the peeling linoleum here felt more welcoming. She took a breath and followed Bode inside.

Something pinched beneath Bode's ribs as he set Harper down and watched her drag Skylar over to a basket of toys.

No woman other than his sister had been here since Isla. And it felt…

Surprising. He'd chewed on the way he might react the whole way here, how it might feel like a betrayal to Isla, but the reality wasn't what he'd expected. And maybe that was a problem.

Because having Sky here felt natural. Normal, almost, like an extension of the relationship they'd been building—

Which was *supposed* to be professional, he scolded himself. Best to cut off this foolish line of thinking and focus on why they were here: to pack their bags and get Harper to Chelsea's.

Sky looked up from where she perched on a chair near Harper's spread of princess dolls. "I'll play with Harper for a bit, if you want to clean up." Her gaze drifted over his filthy clothing, and he laughed.

"You don't want to hang out with me covered in grime?"

"I'd hang out with you regardless." Her cheeks tinted pink. "But your sister might appreciate you more without the dirt."

It didn't take long to make himself presentable and throw together an overnight bag. Harper's things were a little tougher to pack, without knowing how long she'd be away. Chelsea would have even more ammunition now to try to get Harper to stay long-term. He ground his teeth and gathered up a collection of clothing and toys. She'd want her blanket, Lollipop and her other favorite stuffies, too.

When he carried the bags back to the living room, Sky sat with Harper on her lap, studying something. The moisture left his mouth when he realized it was a framed picture—one of the only family portraits they'd taken of the three of them before Isla lost her hair.

"Mommy." Harper pointed at the picture.

“She’s very pretty.” Sky’s tone was tinged with sadness.

“She wiffs in heaven now.”

Sky’s arms tightened around her. “I know, sweetheart. Jesus is taking care of her until you can be with her again.”

Moisture filled his eyes, and he blinked. He’d done his best with Harper over these difficult few years, but seeing her with Sky reminded him of how much more she needed. Maybe as a toddler it hadn’t mattered as much having no mother, but one day soon she’d grow up and wish she had another woman in her life. Yes, she had his sister. She’d have friends and teachers and other adults. But there was no substitute for a mother.

His heart twisted, but the old stabbing grief wasn’t there. Or the thousand *whys* he usually cried out to God. It almost caught him off guard. Was it possible he’d come through the fire, survived and was stronger for it? If anything good had come from Isla’s passing, only the Lord got the credit.

Sky glanced up, as if suddenly aware of him, and he set the bags down next to the door. He’d been so focused on himself and Harper, he hadn’t even considered how strange this situation must be for her. Her near fiancé, with all his money, had surely lived in a much nicer place than this old government housing. And undoubtedly he didn’t carry all this emotional baggage.

No, he was just a jerk.

Bode swallowed, and as their gazes locked, her eyes softened with a warm glow that banished all thoughts of her loser fiancé and the untidy state of his house.

“Looks like you packed. Can I help get Harper ready?”

Right—his bedraggled daughter was still dressed in yesterday’s clothes, with an added layer of filth. And poor Sky had been holding Harper in her lap. The fact she didn’t even seem to notice the dust smudging her clean clothes made his heart warm even more.

"Come to my room!" Harper took Sky's hand and tugged her toward the hall, answering for him. "Find Leepop!"

"I've already got Lollipop packed, sweet pea," he called after them.

While Sky oohed and aahed over all the things Harper wanted to show her, he picked out clean clothes and filled a warm bath for her. When he ushered Harper into the bathroom, Sky pointed back to the living area. "How about I brew us some coffee before we hit the road?"

"Sounds great." Life used to be this way, he and Isla working together as a team. Over the years since he'd lost her, the biting grief had somehow shifted into dull loneliness and the low-level stress of handling everything alone. But now, for this moment, he could almost forget all of that. In fact, since he'd met Sky, there were times he'd almost forgotten about Isla, or put her so far out of his mind that his loss wasn't a conscious thought.

He didn't know what to think about that. Probably he should feel guilty for not honoring her memory, and yet… Sky made him happy, even with all the awful things they'd gone through together. It felt good. Hopeful, like maybe God still had good things for him in this life, not just in eternity.

Harper splashed him with water and giggled, shaking him out of his thoughts. He laughed and dried off his face, then helped her finish getting ready. The warm, rich scent of freshly brewed coffee met his nose as they headed for the kitchen.

Sky had her back to him, rummaging through one of the cabinets. When Harper came skipping up and grabbed her legs, she reached down to tickle her. "Why, you're as shiny and clean as a new penny! All ready for a trip to your aunt's?"

Harper clapped her hands. "Can we bring fishies?" She turned to look at him.

When Bode nodded, Sky held up the bag of goldfish crackers she'd already found. "All packed." She glanced at him. "Do you have any travel mugs?"

"Over here, in the pantry." He pulled open the door to a tall cabinet, wincing as a couple of bags of chips fell out onto the floor. Organizing had been Isla's strength, not his. "Sorry, it's kind of a mess in here. I haven't had a lot of time to clean."

Sky rested a hand on his arm, and her eyes glowed with some hidden emotion. "Bode, it's fine. What you've done here, taking care of Harper alone, it's amazing. I think you've got your priorities straight."

Had the room suddenly gotten twenty degrees hotter? And why was his shirt collar so tight? "Thanks, that's kind of you." He turned back to his messy shelves and dug out an old package of disposable coffee cups with lids. "Here you are. Then let's get this show on the road."

Sky poured the coffee for them, then tidied up the kitchen—a little more sparkly than he ever managed to make it—while he loaded the bags and Harper's backpack full of snacks into the car. After locking up the house, they piled in and headed for the road.

Before he knew it, he was pulling into Chelsea's driveway. The miles had vanished in a blur of conversation and laughter, making his cautious, aching heart feel happier than it had in ages. And every time the nagging voice of reason had popped into his head, demanding he think about what would happen when the case ended or Sky left, he'd ignored it. Later. He'd deal with that later.

"Uncle Bode! Harper!" His niece and nephew came racing down off the porch, and he swept them both into a bear hug before introducing them to Sky. "This is Ethan. He's eight. And Zoe is five."

The children grabbed Harper's hands and dragged her up to the house as Chelsea held the door open. She welcomed them with the same cheerful enthusiasm as always, only this time she checked the subtle look of disapproval she usually bestowed on Bode for insisting he could raise Harper alone.

Instead, she embraced Sky like they were long-lost relatives. "Skylar, I'm so happy to meet you. But of course sorry it's under these circumstances."

"It's nice to meet you, too." Sky pulled back, then glanced between the two of them. "I can definitely see the resemblance."

He laughed. "People always asked if we were twins when we were little."

"But he's the baby, and boy, did he use to act like one." His sister gave his arm a playful swat. Despite their disagreements since Isla's death, they'd always been close. "Tom is at work, but he's looking forward to seeing you."

"Where am I taking this stuff?" Bode held up the bags.

"Harper will share Zoe's room like normal, and Skylar can have the guest room." His sister shrugged. "Which leaves the basement couch for you, Bode."

"Did you kill the spiders this time?" When Sky's eyes went wide, he winked. "It's a joke, don't worry. Chelsea would never permit spiders to live in her house."

"Absolutely not." Chelsea laughed. Nearby, Harper ran in circles with Zoe, squealing. His sister took Harper's hand. "Come on, Harper, let's go put your things in Zoe's room."

He smiled as he watched them go, then showed Sky

where she'd be staying. "Once you're settled, let's go pay a visit to Scott Simmons."

Thirty minutes later, he'd hugged Harper goodbye and climbed back into the car with Sky. As much as he hated to admit it, he really appreciated being able to leave his daughter with Chelsea, where he knew she'd be loved on and cared for. Not that the day care center wasn't great—*usually*—but the teachers weren't family.

He tapped Scott Simmons's address into a mapping application on his phone, then backed the car out of the driveway.

"Your sister seems very sweet."

"She is, most of the time. You know how sisters are." He glanced at Sky, and she laughed. "We've had some battles over Harper, but I'm so thankful she's as close as she is and willing to help out."

He asked Sky about her sister, comparing notes about their experiences growing up, as he followed the directions. Scott Simmons lived on the other side of town, and the buildings became increasingly dilapidated as they drew closer to his address.

"Guess he hasn't done well in life since leaving the climbing scene." Sky's nose crinkled.

"Some guys do great—they take all that determination they poured into climbing and apply it to whatever comes next for them—but others, not so much." He shook his head. "Some can't let the past go. I guess that doesn't apply only to climbers, though."

"No, it definitely doesn't." She grew silent, and he wondered what she was thinking.

He'd certainly spent a long time in the past after Isla died, playing back memories in his mind and stewing in regret that they hadn't caught her illness sooner. Only a sharp kick to the seat of his pants, in the form of Chelsea telling him to get his act together, had allowed him to salvage his relationship with Harper and become the father she so desperately needed.

When they reached the correct address, he parked the car out front on the street. Piles of junk covered the brown lawn near the front of the house, and the roof sagged. A beat-up old Volkswagen van rusted beneath the carport.

"Wait a minute." Sky tugged his sleeve as they walked up the driveway. "That orange van—it looks just like the one in the parking lot at Tuolumne Meadows yesterday."

He snapped a quick picture with his cell phone. Could Scott Simmons have been there?

Sky kept close as they walked on paving stones interspersed with overgrown weeds toward the front door. A large dog barked somewhere nearby, loud and ferocious.

"Let's see if he's home." Bode rang the doorbell, setting the dog off into an even louder volley of barking. When no one came, he rang again.

Finally a voice called from inside. "Hold your horses, I'm coming!"

A moment later, the interior door opened, and an older woman stood facing them on the other side of the screen door. His breath froze.

The woman's hair had gone gray, her skin more wrinkled, but the face that stared back at him looked almost identical to the one he'd seen on his computer screen just the day before.

They'd found Kathryn Hillsburg.

ELEVEN

Sky's mouth went dry as she stared at the woman who had made life so difficult for her mom—and maybe helped a killer fake his own death. Did Bode recognize her? She glanced his way to find his eyes on her, brows slightly raised.

"What do you want?" Kathryn barked. Behind her, the tiny home's living room was packed with clutter and garbage. Empty beer cans on the coffee table, clothing and plastic bags littering the furniture and floor. A TV blared in the background.

"We're looking for Scott Simmons," Bode said. "Is this his address?"

"Yeah, he's here." She turned toward the back hall. "Scott! Visitors." Somewhere in the back of the house, the dog redoubled its efforts to ruin their hearing. "Stupid dog."

"Who is it?" a voice demanded from the back.

She turned to them expectantly.

Neither of them was in uniform, but Bode pulled out his badge and held it up. "I'm with the National Park Service Investigative Services Branch. We'd like to ask him a few questions."

The woman's eyes narrowed. "What's this about?"

"Questions concerning a case." He hadn't mentioned the woman's identity yet; was he afraid of scaring her off?

If she slammed the door in their faces, would they need to get the local authorities involved?

And—the possibility just occurred to her—what if these two knew where Jeremy Flint was? Or were even still colluding with him? Could she and Bode be in danger? A chill swept across her skin, raising goose bumps.

"Scott! It's park rangers!" the woman yelled again, and Sky resisted the urge to cover her ears.

Muffled curses came from the back hallway. Then a man appeared, dressed in a white undershirt with a cigarette hanging from his mouth. He'd lost most of his hair to balding, but his height and build were close enough to her attacker's to make her stiffen.

She took a step closer to Bode, and he shifted his weight toward her. Whatever happened, he would protect her.

"Scott Simmons?" he asked.

"Yep."

Bode showed his badge and identified himself.

Scott held up both hands. "Hey, I ain't been part of the Yosemite scene in years. What's this all about?"

"It's about an old case, Mr. Simmons." Bode tucked his badge back into his pocket. "We hoped you might be able to help."

"I'm not in trouble?"

They both shook their heads, and the man's posture relaxed.

"We're working on a couple of homicides recently uncovered in the park," Bode explained. "We think they might be connected to an old climbing buddy of yours." His gaze flicked to Sky, then back to Scott. "Jeremy Flint. Do you remember him?"

Something clattered behind Scott, and the dog started barking again as the woman swore. Then she pushed her way up beside him, her eyes narrowed. "What's Jeremy got to do with anything? After all I did for him…"

"Kathy, that's enough," Scott snapped. He turned back to them. "We were friends, back in my climbing days. Before I hurt my back and had to quit."

"I'm sorry to hear that, Mr. Simmons," Bode said. "Can you tell me more about Jeremy? Did he have any conflicts with anyone else?"

"Ha." Kathryn snorted, but Scott cut her off with a look. If Jeremy *was* alive, those two seemed to know it—or at the least, they were hiding something.

"Sure, but didn't everyone in those days?" He gave a hollow laugh. "I mean, you get a bunch of single, rowdy, broke climbers together, they're bound to run into trouble once in a while."

These evasive answers weren't getting them anywhere. Sky shifted her weight, and Bode glanced at her, his brows raised. He seemed to be asking her something, but what? She gave the slightest shake to her head.

His gaze lingered a second longer, then he turned back to Scott and Kathryn. "We've been in touch with Jeremy's brother Steven up at Yosemite. He told us about the accident that—" he coughed "—claimed Jeremy's life."

"That was real sad." Scott bowed his head. "A hard loss for all of us."

"Mr. Simmons, do you still climb in Yosemite? We noticed a van like yours up at Tuolumne Meadows yesterday morning."

He shrugged. "That can't be the only orange van in the state."

Too bad she hadn't gotten the license plate number. Finally she could stand it no longer. Maybe Bode had been offering her the chance to interview them. If so, she wanted to take it. She cleared her throat. "Can I ask a question?"

Bode nodded at her. "Of course."

"Ma'am, what did you say your name was? Kathy…?"

"Hillsburg," the woman supplied.

"It's been a number of years, but do you recall the cold case in Yosemite about a missing park ranger? Andy Jansen?" Her father's name felt like thick taffy on her tongue, and her palms grew slick with sweat. To be this close, and yet still not have the answers she wanted, was almost painful.

The woman shrugged. "Maybe."

"A video capture was circulated in the media after his disappearance. It showed you at a gas station with a man who looked similar to Jansen in your passenger seat. The police were unable to track you down at the time."

"I was off the grid." She stuffed her hands into her pockets. "What's it matter now?"

"Who was that man in the passenger seat?"

"Not a park ranger, that's for sure." She let out a cackling burst that grated against every fiber of Sky's being. Bode's hand pressed against her lower back, warm and sturdy. "What difference does it make?"

Well, let's see, the truth would've saved my mother years of silently doubting my father's faithfulness. And right now, it would tell them whether Jeremy Flint was still alive and coming after her.

Bode pulled his hand back and crossed his arms. He looked every inch a tall, serious law enforcement officer, even out of uniform. "We have reason to suspect that Jeremy Flint survived his accident and might have returned to the Yosemite area."

Kathryn inhaled sharply, exchanging a glance with Scott. She shook her head, backing away from the door.

"Don't you tell them nothin' else, Scott. If he knew you were talking to cops..."

Sky's chest tightened. *If he knew...* Had she just confirmed Jeremy was alive?

"Ms. Hillsburg," Bode pressed, "were you one of the EMTs who attended the scene of the Flints' accident?"

She swore again, then swiveled on her heel and disappeared into the dark recesses of the house. The dog resumed its barking, growing louder.

Scott started to shut the door, but Bode held up his hand. "Mr. Simmons—"

"No more questions." The interior door slammed shut, rattling the screen door. The barking kept going, along with indistinct, raised voices. Another door banged.

Sky and Bode exchanged a glance, and he let out a low whistle. "Wow, that was something else."

"I guess we head back to your sister's?"

He nodded. But as she turned to leave, she caught a flash of black coming around the corner of the house. The sound of the barking had suddenly grown a whole lot closer. Her breath caught as she leaned around Bode to see.

A large rottweiler barreled toward the front stoop.

Bode barely had time to step in front of her and throw his arms in front of his face before the dog launched itself into the air.

Heading straight for them.

One hundred and twenty pounds of snarling muscle crashed into Bode, knocking him hopelessly off balance. He fell backward into Sky, and they tumbled off the stoop and into the bushes in a mass of flailing limbs and snapping jaws.

Branches broke and spiked into his back as he landed,

but he used the momentum to shove the dog off to his right. On his other side, Sky scrambled to her feet and pressed against the wall of the house.

The rottweiler growled, lunging for his throat. Bode pivoted his hips, bringing both feet up into the dog's chest and kicking. With a whimper, the dog backed away, though it still growled.

Skylar hammered against the side of the house, her phone in one hand. "Call off your dog before I call the cops!"

Bode stood slowly, keeping both hands out in front facing the dog.

Then a whistle sounded, and the rott's head perked. After a second signal, it turned and raced around the house the way it had come.

A slow breath slipped out as he wiped the sweat from his forehead. Then he turned to Sky. "You okay?"

She nodded, but her knees wobbled as she pushed away from the house. He wrapped her hand around his arm and escorted her back to the car. Once they were safely locked inside, she collapsed back into her seat and turned to him.

"Now what? They clearly know more about Jeremy Flint than they're telling us. And I'm convinced either one of them was at Tuolumne or they loaned that van to Jeremy. What can we do?"

Bode dragged a hand through his hair. "Unfortunately, we have only circumstantial evidence linking them to Jeremy Flint. Nothing that would get us a warrant. All we can do is ask the local authorities to keep an eye on them." At least maybe then they'd know if Scott and Kathryn skipped town. "I'll call the Fresno PD before we drive off. We need to report the dog attack as well. That will help the prosecution if these two end up in court."

Sky fiddled with the hem of her shirt, her attention darting between him and the shuttered house, as he recounted the incident over the phone to an officer. He reached over and placed a hand on her arm, hoping the contact might help ground her.

"Yes, that's the address," he confirmed at the officer's request.

"We'll get someone over there to investigate the dog attack and keep an eye on the house tonight, but I can't promise more surveillance than that," the officer said. "You can either wait for the officer or head downtown to file an incident report."

"We'll wait. I want to make sure they don't drive off as soon as we do." He ended the call, then turned to her. "Looks like we'll be hanging out here a little longer. That okay?"

"Anything to help the case." She double-checked her door was locked, and he squeezed her arm.

Seeing her in danger and afraid like this made his heart hurt. He wished there were some way to shelter her from all of it, to take her away somewhere safe and let her know how valued and cared for she truly was. For a second the intensity of the feeling caught him off guard, so much like the way he'd felt about Isla. He'd thought he would never feel that way about anyone again. And yet…opening up his heart put him at risk to go through all the pain and suffering again as well. What if something happened to Sky?

What if she moved away, as she had already told him she would?

"You okay?" Her soft words channeled into his tumultuous emotions. "Were you hurt?"

He rubbed a hand against his sternum. "Nope, I was just thinking about you." So much for any kind of filter on his mouth. Heat crept up his neck. "How are you holding up?" Maybe she wouldn't read anything into that.

She looked past him toward Simmons's house. "Do you think they know where Jeremy Flint is? She seemed worried someone would find out they were talking to us."

"Maybe." He clenched his jaw. "They're definitely hiding something. And if Jeremy is still alive, as they seemed to imply, where is he living and working? It can't be down here, not with the distance up to Yosemite. When we get back to the park tomorrow, I'm going to reach out to Aramark and some of the other seasonal employers to see if anyone recognizes him."

She nodded, then scrubbed her hands over her face. "I just want all of this to end. And for the truth to be made public, so my family has justice."

Without thinking, he leaned over and pulled her toward him, pressing a kiss to the top of her head. Her hair smelled sweet like almonds and cherry. "I know you do. I want that for you, too. More than I can say."

She trembled beneath his touch, and he wished he could pull her into an embrace and hold her close. But already he'd pushed the boundaries farther than he should. So he released her and settled back into his seat, ignoring the wave of loneliness and longing that threatened to engulf him.

By the time a pair of officers arrived a few minutes later, no one had budged from the house. That was something. If they could prevent these two from running off, they might be key witnesses in the case against Jeremy.

If Jeremy was alive. And if they could find him.

The tangled strands of the case wove themselves into a knot in his brain as he drove Sky back to his sister's house after they'd recounted the incident to the officers on the scene. Chelsea and Tom had left the porch light on for them. When he knocked softly at the door, his sister let them in.

"All the kids are asleep," she said. "I read Harper a story and she snuggled right in."

He raised an eyebrow. "Good to know I'm that easy to replace."

"Replace you?" Chelsea winked. "I wouldn't dream of it."

She glanced at Sky, who shook her head. "There's no replacing you, Bode. Not in that little girl's eyes. You're the hero she needs."

Her words warmed his chest. Maybe he hadn't totally failed Harper.

"You guys must be famished," Chelsea said. "Why don't we head for the kitchen, and I'll get you a plate of leftovers."

His brother-in-law, Tom, waved from the next room. "Pulled pork, right this way!"

Sky's stomach growled, and she cast him a bashful glance before heading toward the kitchen.

His sister lingered, holding him back. She nodded at Sky's retreating form. "Sounds like you've been the hero *she* needs, too."

"Chels…" He rubbed the back of his neck.

"She's very pretty and seems like a sweetheart." His sister's mischievous grin rivaled the Cheshire cat's. "*And* she has a soft spot for Harper."

"Don't start with that. I'm just doing my job."

"Sure, you are."

Two hours later, the house was quiet as he pulled out his laptop on the basement sofa.

What clue were they missing that would make the pieces fit together? Scott Simmons and Kathryn Hillsburg had hinted that Jeremy was, in fact, alive—and he'd have the motive to go after Sky from the moment she saw him burying a body. The fact she was related to his old enemy Andy Jansen was icing on the cake. And with the number of times he'd come after her in the park, he not only knew the area well, but he had to be living close by. Maybe El Portal? Or Wawona?

A thought occurred to Bode, and he opened his case files. What about the woman he'd been burying the day Sky first saw him? How was she connected to Jeremy?

He opened the file, perusing the key data. Sharlene Foxx, twenty-eight years old, from the Bay Area. According to the missing person report filed with the sheriff's office, she'd been staying at Yosemite Lodge when she vanished. Her friends were hanging out in the bar when Sharlene went up to their room early with a headache. Hours later, she was gone.

No sign of forced entry. He chewed the inside of his cheek. That meant whoever had gotten to her had either convinced her to let him in or had a key. Hotel employee? Maintenance worker? Or a man she'd met earlier and was romantically interested in? Whatever had happened, she hadn't counted on losing her life.

Tomorrow after he took Sky back to park headquarters, he'd drive back to the lodge to investigate. Maybe she'd be upset he didn't bring her along, but if Jeremy was there, lurking around that hotel, he didn't want her anywhere near him. She'd be safe with Deputy Moore at the ISB office, researching other possible angles.

And with the Lord's blessing, he'd get the lead he needed to close this case for good. Both for the sake of justice for Sky's family and for the good of his own heart. Because he couldn't keep carrying on like this, growing closer to Sky when there was no way they could be together.

TWELVE

Sky settled into Bode's swivel chair and tried to force her mind onto the task at hand. He'd pulled up the database of park employees, and now her job was to cull through it, checking names and photographs on file for anyone who looked like Jeremy Flint. Of course, they didn't know exactly what he would look like now. There was always the possibility he'd made alterations to change his appearance, but at least they had Steven's facial features as a reference point.

Ultimately, she suspected Bode had found a lead on Jeremy and didn't want to put her in harm's way, which was both thoughtful and annoying at the same time. After what the killer had done to her father and so many other families, she wanted to be there when he was caught.

She glanced at the clock. 11:07 a.m. One minute later than the last time she'd checked. A sigh whooshed out, and she pulled her hair loose from its ponytail and twisted it into a braid instead. After an early breakfast and a quick goodbye, she and Bode had left his sister's house by eight in the morning. Harper had cried and clung to them until Chelsea promised her a trip to the playground and ice cream. Then she'd let go, but her little sniffles had torn at Sky's heart and made Bode extra quiet on the way back.

After he'd gotten her set up at his desk, he'd changed back into uniform and headed out to Yosemite Lodge. And so here she was, doing her best to work while Rachel brewed coffee, and trying to pretend like she didn't miss Bode's solid, reassuring presence.

Her burner phone rang, and she nearly jumped out of her seat at the loud sound. Was it Bode? She'd charged her real phone after they recovered it and found it still worked despite its time in the wilderness. Had he called the wrong number? But when she dug the phone out of her bag, she didn't recognize the caller.

"Hello?"

"Ranger Skylar Jansen?" The man's voice sounded familiar. "This is Steven Flint. We've spoken a few times?"

She sat up straighter. "Right, of course. What can I do for you?" And how had he gotten her number?

"Sorry I had to call your personal number. A ranger at the Visitor Center gave it to me when I couldn't get through to Special Agent Tucker."

Anxiety pinched at her. Surely Bode would've answered his phone if he'd seen a call from Steven. Was something wrong? "Okay. Can I give him a message for you?"

"Actually, I think I might have information that can help you locate my brother."

"Really?" The band around her ribs eased, just a little. If he could help them find Jeremy, this whole thing might actually end. But worry for Bode nagged at her, like a little dog nipping at her heels. What if Jeremy had found *him*, and this information was coming too late? "What is it? Whatever you can tell me will be helpful." Urgency leaked into her voice.

"Listen, I was digging through a drawer of paperwork last night, and I stumbled across an old letter Jeremy had written but never mailed. In it, he mentioned a journal." There was a pause. "Ranger Jansen, from the way the letter is worded, I believe he might've detailed his crimes in the journal. It might provide you some leads to where he is now."

Especially if he was still alive, and possibly even adding to that journal. Her mind whirred. At the least, they'd have an excellent source of evidence to provide the prosecution if and when the case went to trial. "That could be very helpful." She tried to temper her tone. "Can you drop it off here?"

"I'm out with climbers for the day," he said apologetically. "Also, I don't have the journal itself—just a location where he seems to have kept it. Here, let me read this to you." He cleared his throat. *"They say you only live once. Well, I've taken life by the hands, haven't I? Someday when I'm gone, you can read the full story in my Moleskine. Maybe even publish it for me as an autobiography. Steven thought that would help me get in touch with my inner child, but the joke's on him. Anyway, it's buried up at Three Trees if you ever want it."*

"Where is Three Trees?" she asked when he finished. "And who was the letter to?"

"Three Trees is up near Mist Trail. Vernal Falls area? It's not an official place you'd find on a map, just somewhere we used to hang out as kids. The letter was written to his closest friend growing up, but they lost touch. Maybe that's why he never sent it."

She jotted down the information he'd shared. "I will be sure to let Agent Tucker know. Can you give us more precise directions?"

"It's best if I show you in person. My group is heading that way for the afternoon, so I could meet you and Agent

Tucker at the trailhead while they're heading up to the falls. Would forty-five minutes from now work?"

She nibbled her lip. Bode wouldn't be back by then, but Rachel could go with her. And they had a park full of law enforcement rangers she could ask as well. The other options were to wait or ask Steven to find it on his own and drop it off, but both would mean a longer delay. And with the way she'd already put Harper in danger, they needed this case to end.

"Ranger Jansen?"

"I'm here. Yes, that will work. I'll see you then." She clicked off the call, then immediately tapped through to Bode's line. It rang four times before bumping her into voice mail. She hung up, then tried again. On the second attempt, she left a brief message telling him where she was going and why. He'd contact her soon. Right? *Lord, please let him be okay.*

Swallowing her worry, she turned to Rachel, who had just returned to the desk with two mugs of hot coffee. "Thank you," Sky said as she took one. "I hate to do this to you, but we have to run. Steven Flint, our suspect's twin brother, wants to meet us at a trailhead. He's got a lead on some information."

Rachel took one slow, contented sip, then planted the mug on the desk. "I can leave my coffee for the greater good. Let's do it."

"I'll ask Chief Kleinman if a law enforcement ranger can drive us over."

"With the traffic in this park, good call."

Twenty minutes later, their ranger escort had arrived, and they were on their way to the southeast corner of the Valley. Skylar gnawed the inside of her cheek as the ranger inched his way through the traffic. Bode still hadn't returned her call. Most likely he was busy talking to someone—or maybe he had poor cell service—but all the logical reasons did nothing to assuage the concern making her stomach churn.

Finally a parking lot with signage for Vernal Falls and Half Dome came into view. She glanced at her watch—they were five minutes late. Hopefully, Steven would still be there.

"Not again," the ranger groaned. He'd pulled into the lot and promptly stopped behind a line of vehicles. Up ahead, a truck pulling a large camper had gotten stuck while attempting to navigate a corner in the tight lot, and now a stream of cars was backed up like water behind a dam.

She glanced at Rachel. "We can walk from here." When Rachel agreed, she told the ranger, "If you want to help untangle this mess and then wait for us, we shouldn't be long. Or I can call the dispatcher when we're done if you need to leave."

Sky and Rachel climbed out of the ranger's SUV and headed toward the trailhead, passing Steven Flint's fifteen-seater van with the El Capitan Mountaineering logo painted on it, parked in a corner of the lot. She quickened her pace. Off to her right, Glacier Point towered above them, and Half Dome stood to the left. The place she'd first run into the killer, that morning all the trouble started, wasn't far. Goose bumps popped on her skin despite the warm midday sun.

But today was different. The deputy walked beside her, armed, and scores of visitors rambled up and down the trail on their way to some of the park's most popular destinations. No one would be foolish enough to try something out here. And maybe they'd get the information they needed to finally stop Jeremy Flint.

As he'd promised, Steven was waiting at the trailhead next to a placard with route information. His posture was relaxed; he leaned back against a fence, with his hands in his jacket pockets. A small shovel sat propped up next to him. He waved as soon as he recognized Sky.

A crease formed between his brows as she and Rachel approached. “Where’s Special Agent Tucker?”

“He’s tied up elsewhere.” *Hopefully not literally.* The thought hit her with a sharp pang, but she shook it off. Bode knew how to take care of himself—and others, as he’d proven many times already. “This is Deputy Rachel Moore from the county Sheriff’s Office.”

Steven shook hands with her. “I’ve got about an hour and a half before I need to be back down here to wait for my group. We’re heading up the trail for a bit and then off.”

“Sure. Lead the way.” Sky and Rachel followed as Steven started walking, carrying the shovel over his shoulder. Other hikers passed them coming back down from the falls, and the sound of rushing water could be heard in the distance. She chatted with him as they walked, learning that his climbing group had a separate guide who escorted them.

“It’s a great position for me,” he explained. “Gives me lots of free time for other activities, but I still get to be near the climbs I love. It’s hard when you get older and the joints get stiff.” He fisted then opened a hand by way of demonstration.

“No one wants to give up their favorite things,” she said sympathetically. And as she’d learned from her breakup with Chris, you never knew when it would be the last time. She never would’ve imagined when she was getting ready for that dinner, that she’d never go out with him again. Maybe she’d never eat another fancy meal in Manhattan again, either.

Just a few short weeks ago that thought would’ve been physically painful—not because of the loss of fancy dinners, but Chris, and the upheaval of all her expectations. She inhaled a slow breath of clean, mountain air, scented of forest and nearby water from the Merced River. Something had changed since she'd come to Yosemite. Despite all the hard things, God had been slowly working in her, showing her that maybe her plans weren't best. Maybe He had other good things in store for her. The sense of hope warmed her chest and buoyed her spirits as the trail angled more sharply uphill.

Next to her, Rachel was puffing hard with each step. "Can we slow down a little?" She laughed. "I thought I was in good shape until we hit this hill."

Steven glanced back with an apologetic look. "If we do, I won't get back in time." Amazing that for a van driver, he didn't seem winded at all. Even Sky's legs burned. Too bad she hadn't thought to bring some water.

She guessed they'd gone about a mile before he finally stopped to scan the area to the right. Rachel bent over, bracing her hands on her knees but still smiling.

Steven pointed between the trees to the right of the trail. "It's been a while since I've been up here, but this looks right. We'll need to head off the path for a bit to get to the right place."

Sky nodded, then stole a glance at her cell phone. No service up here. If Bode was on his way, how would he know where they'd left the trail? At the last second, she pulled the elastic loop from her hair and wrapped it around a broken branch near the trail. It wasn't much, but hopefully he'd see it. Or maybe she'd be back down the trail before he even arrived.

"You doing okay?" she asked Rachel as they picked their way through the woods after Steven.

The deputy nodded, then tugged at her heavy utility belt

to adjust it. "Probably shouldn't have had all those cups of coffee this morning."

"But you only got a sip before we had to leave."

She grimaced. "Oh, that wasn't my first cup. Not by a long shot."

The going was tough in places where the hillside grew steep. Sky's feet kept slipping on loose pine needles, and Rachel tripped more than once. Only Steven seemed to be sure-footed as a cat, probably because of his years working in the park. Finally, the terrain leveled out, and they stepped from beneath the cover of the trees into a small clearing. Three huge stumps stood in the center in various stages of decomposition.

"Here we are," Steven said. "Three Trees. Jeremy and I used to love climbing on those when we were kids." A muscle twitched in his jaw.

"I'm sorry about your brother," Sky offered. She wasn't sure which would be worse: finding out your twin was a killer or realizing that they were still alive but hadn't told you.

"Me, too." Something hard flashed in his eyes, and for a second, she felt a little shiver track down her spine. But the sun warming the top of her head soon drove it away. Besides, they were here for a reason.

"Where do we need to look for this journal?" Rachel still sounded out of breath, but not as bad as before.

"Anywhere the soil looks disturbed." Steven bent lower, examining one of the stumps. "Or perhaps even in one of the stumps. If he's still alive and has been out here, he would've dug it up to add to it. Then buried it again, or maybe hidden it close by."

Rachel joined him in the center and inspected one of the stumps.

"I'll check the perimeter." Sky ambled along the edge

of the clearing, scanning the ground and nearby foliage. It seemed like an odd place to keep a journal, but then, Steven knew him far better than she did. Or ever wanted to.

"What about down there?" A dozen feet away, Steven pointed to something on the other side of one of the stumps. Rachel bent over to look, and Sky turned her attention back to her own slow path.

Then movement, quick and unexpected, flashed in the corner of her eye. She turned toward Steven just in time to see him raise the shovel. For one horrifying moment, he looked exactly like the killer had that morning in the other clearing, not so far from where they stood. She swallowed the scream trying to escape. He and Jeremy *were* twins, after all. Of course they would look—

He brought the shovel down, but at the last second tilted the blade and swung it.

At Rachel's bent head.

The dull thud reverberated through the clearing and Sky's stricken limbs. She became a statue, frozen with horror, helpless except to watch as Rachel's unconscious—*please, not dead, Lord!*—body toppled over.

Then Steven dived down and stood again with something in his hand.

Her feet unlocked. She opened her mouth, prepared to scream, bolt, dive—she didn't know—until a metallic click stopped her dead in her tracks.

He had Rachel's gun. And he was aiming it right at her.

Bode ground his teeth together as he traipsed back to his park service vehicle, then forced his jaw to relax. Wrecking his enamel wouldn't help solve this case.

The employees at Yosemite Lodge had been more than helpful, going out of their way to provide a list of all staff who had been there at least six months. Many of them were on-site, and he'd spent a solid hour meeting various members of housekeeping, maintenance and the administration. Each time he'd showed them a picture of Steven Flint and asked if they'd seen a similar-looking man.

And each time he'd gotten either a hesitant maybe or a straight-up no.

Jeremy obviously hadn't worked there after all. Which meant Bode had more or less wasted an entire morning, and to top it all off, his cell phone had died.

He yanked the car door open a little harder than necessary and flopped into the seat. *Lord, what am I missing?* Time was running out, and he'd been so certain he'd get a lead on Jeremy at the lodge. Could he work somewhere else close by? Maybe a gas station or mini-mart?

The Fresno police officer assigned to monitor Scott Simmons's house had reported that morning that no one had left. Maybe if Bode could pull together everything they had, he could convince a judge to give them a search warrant for Simmons's home. Or better yet, an arrest warrant for Kathryn Hillsburg for accessory to murder. If they could scare her into talking, maybe she'd fess up to what had happened to Jeremy Flint.

Bode plugged his phone into the in-car charger and backed out of the parking spot. Being away from Sky this long had him worried too, as much as he hated to admit it to himself. Somehow, even though he'd only known her a short time, she'd become a fixture in his life. How was he going to break it to Harper when Sky needed to leave the park after her seasonal employment ended? Or sooner, when the case ended?

His throat grew thick, and he swallowed. As he turned onto the highway leading to the park, his phone sprang back to life with a soft chime. At a red light, he stole a glance at the screen—two new voice mails and three missed calls. His breath stalled. What had he missed?

Using the controls on the steering wheel, he initiated a playback. The first message was from Chief Kleinman. They'd identified the gun found by the visitor in the woods as belonging to Scott Simmons.

Bode tightened his grip on the wheel as the possibilities raced through his mind. Could Simmons be the killer? Or had Jeremy stolen his gun?

Either way, this information should be enough to get a warrant for Simmons's arrest. Then the next message began to play automatically, and Sky's voice filled his car.

He smiled, until he realized what she was saying. Steven Flint had information for her, and instead of waiting for Steven to bring it to the ISB office, she and Deputy Moore were heading out into the field with him.

Worry crackled beneath his skin like an electrical charge. He inhaled slowly through his nose, forcing himself to relax. She wasn't alone. Rachel was with her, and Rachel would be armed. Besides, Steven wasn't the threat; it was his brother, Jeremy.

"Call Skylar Jansen," he told his voice-activated controls.

One ring, two, three, four. Then her voice mail.

"Hey, Sky, this is Bode. Just trying to call you back." He paused, making up his mind in a split second. "I'm heading your way and should reach the trailhead in half an hour."

Good thing he'd driven an official NPS vehicle. As soon as he reached the enormous line to enter the park, he flipped on his emergency lights and skirted the traffic, driving along the shoulder. A half hour would never be enough time to get into the park if he'd had to wait. When he reached the entrance gate, he cut the lights and waved at the ranger on duty. The traffic inside the park wasn't any better, so he kept to the shoulder, only using his lights when he needed to get through sections where cars were blocking his passage.

As he drove, he returned Kleinman's call and told him to forward the information about the gun to Fresno PD. They'd be able to get the arrest warrant, at least for Simmons. He pulled into a ranger-designated space in the Vernal Falls parking lot thirty-five minutes after he'd left Yosemite Lodge. Not bad. After unplugging his cell, he was about to stuff it into his utility belt when the phone rang. The number was for the sheriff's office. Did they have new information?

"Agent Tucker here," he said as he climbed out of his vehicle.

"Bode, this is Deputy Walcott from the sheriff's office. We've been trying to get through to Deputy Moore but haven't been able to."

He locked the vehicle, then stuffed his keys into his pocket. "Yeah, she's out on a trail with Sky. Probably lost cell service." The same thing might happen to him once he went too far, so he forced his feet to maintain a walk instead of running for the trailhead. "What's up?"

"We've got a report back on the fingerprints from the funeral home. For Jeremy Flint?"

His breath caught in his throat. "And?" He swallowed. "Did you find a match?"

"Yes, but not for Jeremy." The deputy paused, and the rest of the world did too as Bode waited. "For Steven Flint."

Bode froze as every cell in his body turned to ice. "What?" Like a computer's blue screen of death, his mental program had crashed and nothing would compute.

"The body the funeral home fingerprinted was Steven Flint." Silence followed, in which Bode couldn't muster an appropriate response. "Agent Tucker?"

Jeremy Flint hadn't died in that accident, just as they'd suspected. But Steven Flint had, which meant…

Jeremy was impersonating his brother. Maybe had been ever since his "death."

And Sky and Rachel had no idea.

Panic lanced through his veins as sharp as knives. Somehow he managed to choke out words, barely aware of what he was saying. "Thanks, I'll let Deputy Moore know."

No wonder they hadn't been able to locate Jeremy. He'd been right there in front of them this entire time, tracking their every move, directing them how he wanted. And right now, he had Sky and Rachel under his control.

His only hope was that the crowds on this popular trail would slow them down. He took off at a run, this time using his radio to call the park dispatcher and request backup. As he shared the information he had, it struck him how precious little he knew.

Jeremy had played his cards well.

Bode ended the call, stashed the radio in his belt, and took off up the trail. Now all he could do was pray he made it before it was too late.

THIRTEEN

Screaming wasn't an option. Not with that gun aimed at her head. Sweat trickled down the back of her neck as Sky lifted her arms. She might be able to dive sideways and get behind cover before he could shoot, but she had no idea how good his aim was. Clearly there were a lot of things she didn't know about Steven Flint.

And Rachel still lay prone at his feet. If Sky ran, he might retaliate by shooting Rachel before coming after her. Shots fired would draw attention from the trail, but they were far enough away it would be too late before help arrived.

"Over here, next to me. Nice and slow." He kept the gun steady.

Sky took a step toward him. If he wanted to kill her immediately, he would've done it already—which meant she had a little more time to find a way to get both her and Rachel out of here alive.

Her pulse jumped with each step as she slowly approached him. When she was within arm's reach, he latched onto her wrist with the wiry strength of a lifelong climber.

Hc stuffed the gun into his waistband and tied her hands together with a length of climbing rope, then shoved her roughly up against a tree face-first. Bark bit into her cheek.

As he wrapped the rope around her back and legs, she twisted her head, searching for Rachel. The deputy lay still on the ground, blood matting her hair to her forehead.

Please let her be all right, Lord.

"You know, this would've gone a whole lot better if you'd just brought Agent Tucker instead of her," Steven said, following her line of sight.

Why? So he could kill them both? Anger warmed some of the ice in her veins. "You're not going to get away with this. Did you kill your brother in that supposed accident? And are you the one who killed my father, too? Then framed Jeremy for everything?"

He cinched the rope around the other side of the tree, yanking so tightly it dug into her back and the tender skin on her calves. From around the other side, as he tied the knot, he laughed.

"You still haven't figured it out, have you? It'll be entertaining to see if Agent Tucker has by the time he gets here." He reappeared from behind the tree, brushing his hands off on his pants, then clipped something to the back of her shirt. "You did tell him where to meet us, didn't you?"

Her eyes went wide as fear crashed through her system. Steven had masterminded this entire situation, hadn't he? And not just to capture her, but to get Bode, too.

And she'd walked right into his trap, endangering both him and Rachel.

"I'll take that as a yes." He smiled, cruel and ugly, then started dragging Rachel out of the clearing. Sky craned her neck until it hurt, trying to see what he was doing.

"Where are you taking her?" And what had he meant about her not figuring "it" out?

He lowered the deputy's limp form to the ground, then straightened. "Setting the trap for Agent Tucker, of course.

I can't have her waking up here." His flat brown eyes landed on Sky, and she wondered how she hadn't noticed the twisted evil in his expression before. "I can trust you not to scream, can't I? Because then I'd be forced to shoot her. Do you want me to shoot her, Ranger Jansen?"

Her throat thickened. What trap was he setting for Bode? Maybe he would use Rachel as bait, leaving her on the trail. Then when Bode stopped to help her, he'd attack. Sharp pain speared her chest almost as if she'd been stabbed. How had they been so blindsided? "You're a monster." She barely choked out the words around the lump in her throat.

"Steven always said so, too." He shrugged, and suddenly it all clicked into place. If she were a cartoon character, a light bulb would've flicked on over her head. They were identical twins.

"You're Jeremy."

"Of course. Did you really think someone could survive that fall off the cliff?" He cocked his head to one side, then shook it. "Well, maybe someone could. But not if they were shoved off without a knot at the end of their rope."

Poor Steven. His twin brother had killed him. "Why? He was your brother."

"Oh, don't get started on that whole '*You must have such a special connection as twins*' nonsense. I've heard it my entire life. But what's the use in having a twin who not only doesn't understand you but actively opposes you? After Carly tried to break up with me and I had to kill her, my brother grew suspicious at her disappearance. Then your father..." His face contorted into an angry mask. "Andy had always had it out for me. Didn't like the way I bent the rules."

"So you killed him?" Her voice broke. "But how did you get him alone?"

"That was the universe getting payback. Wrong place at the right time. He stumbled on me burying Carly's body, almost exactly the way you did with that girl from the hotel, only he didn't get away. But then Steven figured things out after Andy went missing. He threatened to turn me in. So I did my best to placate him, play along with what he thought I should be like. I invited him out for an afternoon of climbing, for old times' sake before I turned myself in." He stared off into the trees, apparently lost in the memory. Then shook himself and smiled. "Well, you know what happened now."

"You killed him, then stole his identity. Kathryn Hillsburg helped you with the cover-up."

"Very good. You're not entirely clueless. Yes, I made sure to pick a day she'd be working. And Scott has proved useful too, in his own way. If he wants his gun back, I left it in the woods after firing at you and Agent Tucker that first day." He rubbed his chin. "Actually, you won't be alive to tell anyone, so don't worry about it."

She wriggled against the tree, testing the tightness of the rope as it chafed her skin. "Why? Why are you doing this? We found Kathryn and Scott in Fresno. It's only a matter of time before they tell the truth."

"I'll be long gone by then. You see, it's time to end this chapter of my life and move on. I left for a while, after Steven's death. I moved away to start fresh, but I couldn't quite let my old life go. I wasn't ready to leave Yosemite and the climbing scene. But you've shown me it's time. I can't live in nostalgia forever. So—" he brushed his hands together "—all I need to do is permanently silence Agent Tucker and yourself, and then I'll be free to go on my way."

Maybe, if she could just keep him talking, Bode would

have time to get here with help. "I don't understand. Why did you kill the others? And why leave the carabiners?"

"Why did I kill the others?" He let out a humorless laugh. "Sometimes you can't help yourself, Ranger Jansen. All I wanted was for a woman to love me, to stay with me, but they didn't want the same thing. I had to teach them a lesson, the way I did to Carly. And the carabiners? A memento so they'd always know who won. Me."

He offered a twisted smile then resumed dragging Rachel. Sky craned her neck until it ached. Rachel's leg twitched, as if she were regaining consciousness. Steven—no, *Jeremy*—stuffed something into her mouth. Then with a loud rip, he tore off a piece of duct tape and fixed it over her face.

Sky relaxed her cheek against the trunk, willing some of the tension out of her stiff neck. For a few minutes she could hear the swishing sound of Jeremy dragging Rachel, then there was nothing but the breeze in the trees and the buzzing of insects. Was he gone? Lying in wait for Bode somewhere along the trail?

She twisted against the tree, fumbling with her fingers against the ropes where they were tied behind her back. If she could untie her hands, maybe she could work her arms out and free herself.

Whistling came from across the clearing, and she froze. Why was he back? Her throat swelled. Had he caught Bode already?

"You know," Jeremy said, approaching her, "it'll be more fun if we wait for Agent Tucker here. Don't you think?"

"I think you're going to fail and—"

He stuffed a wad of dirty fabric into her mouth, so deep she had to resist the urge to gag. "That was a rhetorical question, Ranger Jansen." As she tried to spit it out, he slapped a piece of duct tape, sticky and uncomfortable, across her lips. "There's something so cathartic about it being you. Anyone could've found me, and yet it was you, Andy Jansen's daughter. That day I delivered the flowers and figured out who you were, the whole plan clicked into place. I'm feeling a sense of closure already."

A smile crested his lips, and he inhaled deeply. "Now, you stay here and be a good little piece of bait, and I'll wait right there for your hero to come rescue you." He vanished out of her line of sight around the back of the tree.

She struggled to twist her head in the other direction, scraping her nose against the bark, but Jeremy didn't reappear. Where was he hiding?

Don't come alone, Bode. Please don't let him come alone, Lord. If he showed up with even a second LE ranger, Jeremy would be outnumbered. But then, Jeremy had Rachel's gun and the element of surprise. And maybe other weapons, too. Her breaths came faster and faster. The disgusting rag in her mouth pushed against her tongue, suffocating her, until lights flickered on the edges of her vision.

Breathe. But it wouldn't work now to tell herself she was safe. She *wasn't* safe. Neither was the man she'd come to care about so much over these intense few days. Still, she forced herself to inhale a slower, deeper breath through her nose. They weren't dead yet. God was with her, and He was in control. And in the most important sense, she *was* safe. She belonged to Him body and soul, in life and death, and so did Bode. Whatever happened in this life, God wouldn't abandon her.

The blackness receded from the edges of her vision. How far away was Bode now? She had no doubt he would come, and knowing him, probably by himself because he wouldn't want to wait for backup. In fact, why *would* he call for backup? He had no idea Steven was actually Jeremy.

Her pulse hammered again, and her breath came too fast and sharp. The sense of suffocation returned, and along with it came the deep-seated urge to dissolve into utter panic.

No. She couldn't give in to that feeling, couldn't give up. Working her hands again, she twisted her wrists, trying to loosen the rope.

Bode was walking into a trap, and she was the only one who could warn him.

Sweat dripped down the sides of Bode's face, and his shirt clung to his back as he hustled up the crowded trail. Families with young children stopped to pull out snacks, creating a traffic jam, and descending hikers flowed in a steady stream in the opposite direction. Time ticked past in a blur of footsteps and exertion.

How far up the trail had Jeremy taken them before turning off? Sky's directions in her message were vague at best, and "Three Trees" wasn't on any park map. At least he knew they'd be turning off to the right, because the left led to the river only a short distance away, where they would be easy to spot. Jeremy would lead them off-trail, away from the crowds.

Bode scanned the edge of the trail as he hiked, searching for broken foliage or footprints or any other indication where they'd gone. Frustration built beneath his skin, a dull, fizzing sensation that amplified his discomfort from the heat. This search was taking too much time. Sky could already be—

No. He clamped down on the thought before it could fully form. *Please protect her, Lord.* After what he'd gone through with Isla... *Lord, I can't do that again. Please.* God had been faithful and gotten him through the storm, and He would continue to be with him no matter what. But he couldn't think about losing Sky.

A flash of turquoise caught his eye, and he paused. Someone had tied something to a branch, right near head level. When he inspected it more closely, he realized it was a hair loop, the kind Sky wore to tie her hair back. Had she left it for him? Did she suspect the truth?

The ground bore evidence of recent trampling to the right of the trail, just before the branch she'd marked. How long ago had they passed through here? His mouth went dry, and he swallowed. *Please protect her, Lord. And Deputy Moore, too.*

Birds twittered in the trees, and a breeze carried the cool scent of earth and summer foliage. On the trail, visitors chattered and stopped to take pictures. All of it felt brutally at odds with what was happening. He headed off the trail, watching for broken sticks, trampled grass and other evidence that they'd passed that way. The entire process was painstakingly slow, and more than once he had to backtrack—but it appeared they were heading perpendicular to the trail, keeping along a wide ridge.

Up ahead, a glint of gold in the sunlight caught his eye, and he hurried his pace. The woods around him were silent as he bent over to pick it up. A star-shaped badge from the sheriff's office. Deputy Moore's? He dragged a hand over his face. *Please, God.*

The prayer came more as emotion than words, as if his spirit was crying out directly to God, bypassing his brain. He rushed on, scrambling over fallen logs and skirting denser patches of undergrowth. Sky's name pounded through his mind with each step. They'd only known each other a few days, and yet she'd grown to be a key piece of his existence. And Harper—despite all his efforts to keep Harper from getting attached, she cared about Sky as much as he did.

Maybe even...one day...love?

The depth of his emotions stunned and thrilled and sobered him all at once. But now wasn't the time to think about it or what it meant. Now he had to get to her before it was too late.

Up ahead, sunlight streamed thick and golden between the trees. By his best reckoning, he'd walked maybe half to three-quarters of a mile from the trail. Was this the Three Trees clearing?

As much as he wanted to charge ahead, he slowed his pace, fingers drifting toward the gun in his utility belt. Maybe Jeremy was still playing his game, pretending to be Steven. Maybe he didn't know Bode had figured out the truth yet. He could use that fact to his advantage. When he didn't hear anything unusual, he kept going, closer to the edge of the clearing. Three huge stumps stood in the center, broken off at about waist height. The collapsed trunks must've decayed or been hauled off years ago.

Then he saw her, tied up to a tree on the opposite side of the clearing. Jeremy had bound her hands behind her back, then lashed her face-first against the trunk. A bright red carabiner dangled from the back of her shirt, a silent threat.

A pit opened in his stomach, and it took all his self-control not to race directly to her. *Thank You, Lord, that she's still alive.* Jeremy had revealed his hand, but what card would he play next? Bode couldn't afford to not be cautious.

He paused on the edge, still beneath the cover of the trees. There was no sign of Rachel or Jeremy. And although

Sky appeared to be wrestling with the ropes binding her hands, she hadn't seen or heard him.

What would he do, if he were Jeremy? Probably lie in wait somewhere farther up the trail, where he could catch him by surprise. But Jeremy hadn't been there.

Was he the type that enjoyed a show? Maybe he was hiding here, ready for Bode to appear in the clearing and attempt to rescue Sky. And what about Rachel? Had he stashed her somewhere nearby? For now, Bode had to assume she was incapacitated somewhere, which meant Jeremy had access to her weapon, in addition to whatever else he'd brought.

Nothing moved in the clearing besides Sky's fingers as she worked at the ropes. Could he linger here, waiting for backup? Or would Jeremy grow impatient and simply shoot her? Tendrils of fear snaked through Bode's veins, and he gritted his teeth. He couldn't just stand here and do nothing.

He took a step to his left, then paused, listening. When he didn't hear anything, he kept going, working his way along the edge of the clearing to where Sky still struggled with the ropes on her hands. A stick snapped beneath his feet, and he froze.

She jerked her head in his direction, studying the shadows. A pang of worry flickered through him at the sight of the scraped skin on her face. When he waved, her eyes went wide, and she shook her head. Still no sign of Jeremy. Was it possible he *was* somewhere along the trail, and Bode had avoided him?

It would only take a moment's work to cut through that rope binding her to the tree. Quietly he reached into his utility belt and pulled out a pocketknife. He'd have to sheath his gun to use the knife, so he slid it back into the holster and eased open the blade.

He took a single step out from the shadows, pausing in the bright sunshine. Waiting for a gunshot. When nothing happened, he kept going, one slow step at a time.

Sky whimpered softly as he reached for her hands, squeezing her fingers briefly before letting go. Now to get through these bonds as quickly as he could. He tugged on the rope to create a little slack, then worked the blade underneath, sawing rapidly. It'd be easiest to release her from the tree first and get her hands afterward.

With a rough, scratching sound, she turned her head again to look the other way. He wanted to offer her some comfort, tell her the rope was starting to tear, but he didn't dare make any extra noise. Almost there—

A muffled scream came from her. He jerked his head up just as a dark figure lunged from behind the cover of a nearby tree. At nearly the same instant something slammed into his knee. Fiery pain shot up through his leg, and he lost his balance. The knife slipped from his grasp as he crashed to the ground.

Then Jeremy was above him, a raised shovel in his hands, swinging it toward Bode's head like he wanted to decapitate him. Bode twisted out of the way, grabbing the other man's legs and yanking him down to the ground. The shovel went flying. They rolled across the ground, each struggling to get the upper hand, and Bode's knee cried out in protest each time he put pressure on it.

"Bode!" Sky called, and he realized she'd worked herself loose.

Jeremy realized it, too. Rage etched itself across his face. He darted a hand toward the gun in Bode's holster but came away empty when Bode shoved him off. Then suddenly he was on his feet, diving for Sky instead.

She was far smaller than Bode and not expecting the attack. Before Bode could react, Jeremy had pinned her to the ground, his fingers wrapped around her throat. "You will not steal this ending from me," he said, his voice hoarse.

Sky struggled to fight him off, and red seared across Bode's vision. He didn't draw the gun, didn't dare attempt to shoot when Jeremy was so close to her. Instead Bode grabbed the shovel off the ground.

"Get off her!" he roared. When Jeremy ignored him, Bode gritted his teeth and brought the flat of the blade down on the other man's back.

Jeremy collapsed forward, landing on Sky, but his grip on her throat loosened enough that Bode could shove him off. He dropped the shovel and pulled his gun.

"Don't move or I'll shoot!"

A twisted smile crept across Jeremy's mouth, and he pushed again toward Sky, where she lay massaging her throat. Bode aimed for his midsection, exhaled and pulled the trigger. The noise of the blast ricocheted through the clearing, making Sky scream. The smile vanished off Jeremy's face, and he curled into a fetal position.

Bode holstered the gun and reached for Sky, tugging her out of the other man's reach. Voices echoed from across the clearing, and he looked up to see Chief Kleinman and Jace Rivera racing out from beneath the trees with three or four more rangers.

Thank You, Lord. A shudder racked his body. He slumped to the ground and pulled Sky toward him. Her face was pale, and her hair hung in clumps against scraped cheeks. Purple bruises were already forming around her neck. But her eyes, her gorgeous gray-green eyes, stared up at him with glossy, unshed tears.

Suddenly he couldn't breathe. He reached for her, running a thumb across her cheek to catch a tear. She blinked, a soft smile on her lips. "You came."

"Of course. I'll always come for you." *Always.* The word resonated to his core. "Are you all right?"

She sniffled, nodding, then looked over her shoulders. "Where's Rachel?"

Right. Now was *not* the time for indulging in feelings. He climbed to his feet, then nearly fell again when he tried to place weight on the bad knee.

"Bode?" Alarm ringed Sky's voice, and she draped his arm around her shoulders.

Jace appeared on his other side, looking him up and down. "Hey, man, glad to see you. Let's get you over here." Together they helped him over to the lowest stump, where he could half sit, half lean against it. Chief Kleinman and another LE ranger had taken Jeremy Flint into custody, along with providing first aid measures to address the gunshot wound to his abdomen.

"Deputy Moore is out here, too. He tied her up and carried her off, that way I think?" Sky pointed into the woods, then wrapped her arms around her stomach. "I hope she's okay."

"We'll find her," Kleinman assured them. He gave orders to the other rangers, then turned back to Bode and Sky. "Are you two all right?"

She glanced at Bode with a tender expression that melted his insides like butter on hot toast. "Thanks to Agent Tucker." Her gaze lingered a moment before she turned back to the chief and Jace. "That's Jeremy Flint. Apparently he killed his twin brother, then stole his identity."

Jace's eyebrows lifted. "Was he the one you interviewed? Burke's gonna want to hear this."

Bode nodded. "He's been living in the area for the

last several years, driving for one of the mountaineering schools. Once we figure out where he went between his supposed death and when he moved back, we might be able to solve more cases." Jeremy had probably left a trail of victims wherever he moved.

"How did you figure it out?" Sky asked him. "I didn't until he admitted it to me. I thought we were wrong about Jeremy and that Steven was the killer."

"Fingerprints from the funeral home. They came back as Steven's." He glanced at Kleinman. "I hope Fresno PD bagged Simmons and Hillsburg. Those two must've helped him out."

"Jeremy told me he had Simmons's gun that first day," Sky said. "He left it in the woods."

"Correct. That's the one the visitor found. Officers were en route to their address last time I checked," the chief replied. "And my rangers who evaluated the rockfall that nearly buried you the other day confirmed it appeared to be caused by a small explosive."

Bode clenched his jaw. How close they'd come to not making it, and yet God had protected them. Rangers stepped back into the clearing nearby, with Rachel propped up between them, and the tension lingering in his spine washed out of him.

"Rachel!" Sky rushed over to her, giving her an impromptu hug. The deputy squeezed her back.

A medical team arrived a few minutes later and hoisted Jeremy Flint onto a stretcher. After assessing the area's accessibility, Chief Kleinman elected to call in a helicopter to evacuate the injured man. When it arrived, he insisted Bode, Sky and Rachel go as well rather than hike back down.

He could barely make the step up into the chopper. Now

that the adrenaline was wearing off, his knee throbbed brutally, and the swelling made it hard to bend.

Sky sat next to him, a worried look on her face as she studied him. But instead of saying anything, she took his hand and held it. He tilted his head back and let the comfort of her touch and the rhythmic noise of the rotors lull him into sleep.

FOURTEEN

Sky stared out the window of the medical center's waiting room, then pivoted and resumed her pacing. Good thing no one else was here, or she'd be driving them nuts. Both she and Rachel had been treated for minor scrapes and dehydration, but after a couple of hours of observation, they'd been released. Rachel had been given strict instructions to take a few weeks off for a concussion after Jeremy's blow to her head, and when a fellow deputy arrived to give her a ride, Sky had hugged her tightly one last time.

"Thank you for everything."

Rachel laughed, then winced and rubbed her head. "I'm not sure I did much besides acquire a massive headache, but you're welcome."

"You made me feel safe during the most dangerous time in my life."

The deputy smiled. "I'm honored that I could help. And it was wonderful to meet you, Sky. If you decide to stick around Yosemite, let me know and we can go for a hike sometime. *Without* a killer."

"I'd like that." She had waved goodbye, then watched through the glass as Rachel climbed into a squad car.

And now she was here alone, waiting for news on Bode. All she'd heard was that he was in surgery for a fractured kneecap, but that had been two hours ago when she was released. Jeremy had been flown to a larger hospital in the nearest city, where he was undergoing surgery also.

She stopped mid-pace as the front doors opened and Chief Kleinman entered with Agent Rivera.

"Any word?" Kleinman asked.

"Just that he's in surgery." She stuffed her hands into her pockets to prevent herself from fidgeting. After all they'd gone through, she wanted to be with him. To sit and talk, to process. Maybe just to hear his voice and see that kind smile lighting up his strong face. Warmth filled her, but doubts gnawed away at the edges of her happiness.

The thought of losing him had been crushing. The thought of moving away now was equally crushing. She wanted to be a part of his and Harper's lives…but would he be willing to take the risk of letting her in?

She hoped so, and the way he'd looked at her back in the clearing had buoyed her insides like a hot-air balloon. But now that they were back in the Valley and had to think ahead about real life, maybe he wouldn't be interested. Her heart hurt, and she rubbed a hand over her sternum.

"There's the man of the hour!" Jace said, and her gaze snapped to the main hallway. Bode hobbled out on a pair of crutches next to a nurse, a knee immobilizer wrapped around his leg.

"He insisted on walking instead of using a wheelchair," the nurse said apologetically.

Bode shrugged. "Can't waste time getting started on my recovery." His gaze landed on Sky, and her imagination filled with all the things they could do together—hiking and climbing, taking Harper for a picnic, watching the sunset.

Her cheeks warmed, and Jace laughed. "Dude, you're making her blush."

Bode leaned on his crutches, rubbing the back of his neck, but his eyes didn't leave her face. Was there a chance he shared these same feelings? That he'd be willing to give a relationship between them the opportunity to grow?

The nurse interrupted the moment with a list of care instructions. She handed the sheet to Bode, then turned a sharp glance on the chief ranger. "Are you his employer? He needs adequate time off to rest and let that knee heal."

The chief chuckled. "I'll be sure to tell Agent Henlow."

Pink and orange had streaked the sky by the time they left the medical center. The next days passed in a blur of reports and statements and documentation for the case. No time to catch her breath or have a word alone with Bode. And as the time passed, she couldn't help thinking maybe she'd read the situation wrong. Maybe it would be better for her to return to Manhattan and try to rebuild her life there.

Maybe Bode and Harper were better off without her.

A burning pit formed in her stomach like an ulcer. New York didn't feel like home anymore. And now that her family had finally found closure regarding her father, the thought of living closer to her mom in southern California or her sister in Missouri was appealing. But once her seasonal position here ended, what kind of job did she even want? These decisions had seemed so far off back in Manhattan when she applied for the position in Yosemite, but suddenly her life choices were front and center.

She sat in the front row of a press conference set up in the Visitor Center auditorium, listening as Bode, Chief Kleinman and the sheriff took turns fielding questions about the case. They'd been able to put to rest the rumors circulating about her father's disappearance, as well as confirm that Jeremy Flint had been taken into custody and that his brother Steven was the one who had died in the accident years prior. Kathryn Hillsburg and Scott Simmons had been arrested too under accessory-to-murder charges, although Bode thought they'd take a plea bargain.

When the questions ended and the reporters finally drifted away, she stood. She'd put off her decisions long enough. It was time to go chat with her supervisor and discuss how the rest of her time at Yosemite would look. Her gaze drifted to Bode, but he was deep in conversation with the chief ranger. She swallowed, then headed for the center aisle.

Bode watched Sky leave her seat, wishing he could detach himself from Kleinman and run after her. But was that the best course? Did she *want* to stay in Yosemite and be part of his life, or was he deluding himself?

The last several days had been incredibly intense, more so than almost any other time in his life. Maybe these heady feelings for her wouldn't last. He balled his hand into a fist, and his fingernails dug into his palm. Was that a risk he wanted to take?

"Miss Sky!" A tiny, very familiar voice echoed from the back of the auditorium. Kleinman was still talking to him, but Bode couldn't help looking up. His sister waved from the back of the room, and there was Harper, sweet and innocent and safe. Her blond curls bounced around her cheeks as she danced down the center aisle right toward Sky.

Sky stooped low and held out both arms, sweeping his daughter up into a hug. She twirled around and Harper giggled. The look of sheer bliss on her face wiped away any doubts he'd had. This brave, strong, caring woman loved his daughter—and she'd be the role model Harper needed so badly. Besides, he knew beyond a doubt that Isla would approve.

His eyes burned, and he blinked. The question was, did Sky care for him anywhere close to as much as he cared for her? Could she see herself with him—long-term?

Forever. Any other time frame wouldn't be enough time with Sky.

"I'm sorry, Chief, I've got to run." He cut Kleinman off mid-sentence, but the older man glanced between him and Sky and smiled.

"Go on with you." The chief gave Bode a friendly nudge. "We can talk later."

With these crutches, hustling was out of the question. He hobbled over to the steps, gingerly easing himself down and trying not to fall. Graham Burke, who'd sat in on the session, rushed over to give him a hand.

"Thanks, Burke." He grunted. "It's rough having the bum knee."

"Especially when you need to get to your girls." He winked, then nodded toward Sky and Harper.

Heat crept up Bode's neck, and he shook his head at Graham before working his way in front of the stage toward the aisle. Sky set Harper down, then turned to watch him. Her smile lit up her whole face.

"Daddy!" Harper came running toward him, and Sky trailed after, tugging the little girl's hand.

"Be careful with Daddy, Harper. He hurt his knee."

He longed to swoop her up but had to settle for patting her little head as she threw her arms around his good leg. "Daddy, me missed you and Miss Sky." She pressed her face into his leg, muffling her voice.

"We missed you too, sweet pea." He glanced up at Sky, checking for her reaction. Had he said or implied too much? But only the loveliest, most tender smile graced her face.

He held out a hand to her, balancing with the crutch beneath his arm.

She stepped forward and took his fingers in hers.

"Stay?" he said softly.

Her throat bobbed, and she blinked away the sheen in her eyes.

"I'm not very eloquent about feelings." He glanced down at Harper, then back up to her. "I didn't think I'd ever feel this way again after Isla, but somehow you swept into my life, and I can't imagine you not being part of it. Part of our life. So will you stay and see where this goes?"

She smiled, warm and beautiful. Then nodded, and his heart threatened to burst out of his chest. "Yes. I'll stay."

Harper squealed, then ran over to hug Sky again. "Be my new mommy?"

Heat exploded in Bode's face. His daughter had just proposed. And as much as *he* wanted to, they needed a firm foundation first. Time to get to know each other apart from the chaos of the last several days, to make sure God was leading them in the same direction. Though he had a pretty good gut feeling right now.

Sky laughed. "Maybe one day. For now, I just want to spend time with you and your daddy." Her eyes met his, and happiness flooded every inch of his being.

EPILOGUE

December, seven months later

"Okay, you ready, sweet pea?" He and Harper had gone over the plan at least a hundred times, but getting a four-year-old to cooperate wasn't always the easiest task.

"Yes, Daddy." Harper stared shyly down at the note in her hand, then fluffed the layers of her bright red dress. "When is Miss Sky coming?"

He glanced at his watch, then froze as a sense of panic threatened to swallow him whole. "Ten minutes." The words came out in a squeak, and he struggled to draw in a deep breath.

"Bode, let me help." Chelsea appeared from the back hallway and joined them behind the counter. He'd spent weeks agonizing over the right place for a proposal, and in the end had chosen here, the Visitor Center. Off-season and after hours, the place was empty except for himself, Harper and his sister and brother-in-law and their kids. Chief Kleinman had happily given his permission.

A tall Christmas tree with thousands of twinkling lights stood in the front corner. Chelsea had helped him place electric tea lights on every horizontal surface until the entire room glowed. And one of his colleagues knew a guy in hospitality who'd provided a beautifully set table for seven and a multicourse meal, kept hot over burners until they were ready.

"Chels..." Bode straightened. "What if she says no?"

"Then you and me and Tom and the kids will enjoy a nice dinner anyway." She rolled her eyes. "Bode Tucker, she is *not* going to say no. That woman is head over heels gone for you. Anyone with a pair of eyeballs can see it."

Sky had applied for and gotten one of the rare full-time park service positions that wasn't in law enforcement. She'd been able to stay in her small apartment, and she and Bode had spent every spare minute together. His knee had finally mended, and he looked forward to taking her climbing again when spring returned to the Valley.

Jeremy Flint had recovered well enough to stand trial. Bode and the sheriff's office had continued the investigation, eventually finding concrete evidence linking Jeremy to the deaths of all four Yosemite victims. With the help of the local authorities, they'd also discovered two more female homicide victims in Nevada, where he'd worked at a climbing gym for a few years between his stints in Yosemite. Jeremy's conviction in Harper's abduction, as well multiple counts of homicide, had been unanimous, and he'd been sentenced to life in jail without parole. During the trial, Bode had gotten the chance to meet Mrs. Jansen, along with Sky's sister Addie and her family. The rift between Sky and her mother was deep, but he hoped that Sky's relationship with her would only strengthen as time passed.

Chelsea straightened his tie. "Everything's ready. Let me stay back here with Harper, and then I'll nudge her out when it's the right moment. Okay?"

He nodded, mostly because Sky would be there any minute, and he was too much of a wreck inside to argue. Chelsea slipped back behind the counter and ducked out of sight, and he positioned himself in front of the table to wait.

Then Sky was at the door, pulling it open and gasping in delight as she took in the soft glow of the space. She wore an emerald-green dress that fit her perfectly and made her hair radiant. When her gaze landed on him, a cascade of butterflies let loose in his stomach, and the ring in his pocket seemed to weigh a thousand pounds.

She tilted her head. “It’s beautiful in here.”

“Not nearly as beautiful as you.” He could barely get the words out through the lump swelling in his throat. As cheesy as the line sounded, it was the pure truth. “Before we eat, there’s a little girl here with a question for you.”

“Harper?” Sky’s eyebrows shot up, and she giggled.

Right on cue, Harper came skipping out from behind the counter. She ran to Bode, who picked her up. Then she opened the paper they’d prepared together earlier that day. Harper’s drawings of rainbows and hearts surrounded the words he’d carefully written for her: *Miss Sky, will you be my new mommy?*

Time froze as he waited, watching the motion of her eyes as she read the message. Then her whole face lit up, her gaze flicked back to his face and the candles and the Visitor Center vanished. There was nothing but Skylar Jansen and the warmth filling his entire being.

“Really?”

“Really.” He set Harper down, then lowered himself onto one knee, fumbling in his pocket. His fingers latched on to the case, and he opened it, holding it up before her. “Skylar Jansen, you have my whole heart. I want to spend the rest of my life with you. Will you marry me?”

She pressed her hands together, then lifted them to her

mouth. Her eyes turned glossy, and she blinked, then nodded. "Yes. Of course, yes!"

Behind him, Chelsea clapped and called for Tom. He and Ethan and Zoe came out from their hiding place in the hall, cheering.

Bode slipped the ring onto Sky's finger and pulled her close. As Harper danced around their legs and his family cheered, joy filled him to the brim. He pressed his mouth to Sky's in a soft kiss, the first of many in a lifetime of God's blessings to come.

* * * * *

Dear Reader,

Thank you so much for picking up Bode and Sky's story. I hope you enjoyed spending time with them and sweet little Harper as much as I did. When I was brainstorming settings for my next book, I knew I had to pick the scenic wilderness of Yosemite National Park. The stunning granite cliffs and waterfalls make the perfect backdrop for a romantic suspense story.

Both Bode and Sky have gone through their share of past heartache. Life doesn't always work out the way we planned, does it? As they wrestle with their growing feelings, they must choose whether to open their hearts to the possibility of good things or stay closed off. That can be a tough choice. When we've already been hurt, how do we find the strength to take the risk of being hurt again?

Thankfully, like Sky and Bode, we have a loving Father who holds us close in His hands. No matter what life throws at us, He treasures us and promises to walk with us each step of the way. Even if we don't get that happy ending in this life, we are guaranteed our Happily-Ever-After with Him in heaven through Jesus. I pray that wherever you are today, you'll find hope and encouragement in His great love.

I love hearing from readers! Keep in touch (and sign up for my newsletter) through my website, www.kellievanhorn.com.

Blessings,

Kellie VanHorn

Get up to 4 Free Books!

We'll send you 2 free books from each series you try PLUS a free Mystery Gift.

Both the **Love Inspired®** and **Love Inspired® Suspense** series feature compelling novels filled with inspirational romance, faith, forgiveness and hope.

YES! Please send me 2 FREE novels from the Love Inspired or Love Inspired Suspense series and my FREE gift (gift is worth about $10 retail). I may cancel anytime by emailing ReaderServiceInfo@Harlequin.com or by calling 1-800-873-8635. If I don't cancel, I will receive 6 brand-new Love Inspired Larger-Print books or Love Inspired Suspense Larger-Print books every month and be billed just $7.19 each in the U.S. or $7.99 each in Canada. That is a savings of 20% off the cover price. It's quite a bargain! Shipping and handling is just 75¢ per book in the U.S. and $1.75 per book in Canada.* I understand that accepting the free books and gift places me under no obligation to buy anything—they are mine to keep for free no matter what I decide.

Choose one: ☐ **Love Inspired Larger-Print** (122/322 BPA G3CD) ☐ **Love Inspired Suspense Larger-Print** (107/307 BPA G3CD) ☐ **Or Try Both!** (122/322 & 107/307 BPA G3CE)

Name (please print)

Address Apt. #

City State/Province Zip/Postal Code

Email: Please check this box ☐ if you would like to receive newsletters and promotional emails from Harlequin Enterprises ULC and its affiliates. You can unsubscribe anytime.

Mail to the **Harlequin Reader Service:**
IN U.S.A.: P.O. Box 1341, Buffalo, NY 14240-8531
IN CANADA: P.O. Box 603, Fort Erie, Ontario L2A 5X3

Want to explore our other series or interested in ebooks? **Visit www.ReaderService.com or call 1-800-873-8635.**

*Terms and prices subject to change without notice. Prices do not include sales taxes, which will be charged (if applicable) based on your state or country of residence. Canadian residents will be charged applicable taxes. Offer not valid in Quebec. This offer is limited to one order per household. Books received may not be as shown. Not valid for current subscribers to the Love Inspired or Love Inspired Suspense series. All orders subject to approval. Credit or debit balances in a customer's account(s) may be offset by any other outstanding balance owed by or to the customer. Please allow 4 to 6 weeks for delivery. Offer available while quantities last.

Your Privacy — Your information is being collected by Harlequin Enterprises ULC, operating as Harlequin Reader Service. For a complete summary of the information we collect, how we use this information and to whom it is disclosed, please visit our privacy notice located at https://corporate.harlequin.com/privacy-notice. Notice to California Residents—Under California law, you have specific rights to control and access your data. For more information on these rights and how to exercise them, visit https://corporate.harlequin.com/california-privacy. For additional information for residents of other U.S. states that provide their residents with certain rights with respect to personal data, visit https://corporate.harlequin.com/other-state-residents-privacy-rights.

LIRLIS2603